FAITH PHYSICS

FAITH PHYSICS

An Introduction to the
Science of the Afterlife

Andrej Bičanski

This book is written in British English.

Cover design by Søren Bendt Pedersen
www.sorenbendt.com

Layout design by Maria Fernandez Marinovic
www.fernandez.com.uy

To all who selflessly set
themselves up as targets of satire

Table of contents

Preface

Faith Physics - An Introduction to the Science of the Afterlife was published in its original form in 2030. Roughly eight years have passed since I wrote the first iteration. It started out as an introductory text to the annual collection of academic articles discussed at the meetings of the International Society for Snesenology, where academics discussed the cutting edge of the science of the afterlife. Although it aimed to be accessible to scholars from a large variety of fields, interested laymen, and even the general public, it was never intended as a work of popular science. Yet, in the years since its first publication as part of a collection of otherwise highly technical papers, it has attracted a large following. It has become an indispensable guide for the educated public, a prerequisite for anybody who wishes to discuss the peculiarities of faith physics and its consequences for society. In retrospect this may not be surprising. Without a minimum of guidance, some of the things we have learned through our conversations with the departed are hard to come to terms with.

I have expanded the text every year since its first publication, and it has finally reached the stage where it has become too large to fit into a collection of research papers. In particular, I have included introductory chapters on the early developments of Faith Physics and on its founder, Alfred Louis Snesenon. But the reader should not be mistaken. This is not the story of one person. It is rather the story of the discipline he created and how it affected all our lives.

The present edition, although separated from its origins, preserves many of the idiosyncrasies of an academic work. In particular, I have kept references to on-going research and citations of academic articles in the text. Hopefully this will allow the reader to appreciate the context in which the original text was written. Enthusiasts may even go on to read some of these articles after finishing this introduction. Nevertheless, I have endeavoured to make the original text more accessible by expanding it here and there and by including many explanatory notes.

The uninitiated reader should be aware that faith physics is, by any standards, a young scientific theory. Most of its empirical observations have not yet found their place in a unified theoretical framework. Consequently, the text focuses on a historical account of the subject, recounting the crucial discoveries in roughly chronological order, yet embedding them in a coherent narrative. Grand theories, which aim to explain all our observations concerning the hereafter, are only beginning to emerge. The present edition is the first to contain an account of exciting new developments. Scholars (including myself) have devised first rudimentary theories, which propose solutions to some well-known problems of faith physics, such as the common sense paradox and the final frontier of faith.

Finally, and by popular demand, this updated edition contains a brand new final chapter, which addresses what some readers mistakenly see as a bleak outlook painted by modern faith physics. Breaking with the otherwise sober style of this work, it outlines a positive manifesto, allowing us to fully appreciate the magnificence of a universe in which humanity has proven beyond any reasonable doubt that life after death is an empirical reality.

London, April 2037.

01

Quantum Soul Theory

In the year 2022 life after death became a real thing. This is, of course, a figure of speech. The beyond has always been a reality. Of this we can be certain, for in this essay I give an account of how humanity has discovered incontrovertible empirical proof for the afterlife, the hereafter, or (perhaps) heaven.

The present text is based on the introductory chapter of the Proceedings of the International Society for Snesenology (ISS). Some of the academic writings found in the Proceedings, and others cited in this text, may be hard to follow, but the present work is devoted to interested laymen and members of the general public.

It is a great honour and privilege to have been given the task of writing this introduction. To disseminate the fruits of this scientific revolution to the wider public is a matter that is very close to my heart. In the following chapters I will try to give a thorough yet understandable overview of how we discovered irrefutable proof for the afterlife and how this monumental discovery changed the world. I have endeavoured to make this introduction accessible and to structure it in such a way as to bring the interested reader up to speed on the current hot topics of the field, while at the same time devoting enough space to an account of the most interesting research of the past decades. It will—I hope—also prepare some of you for a reading of scholarly articles.

The attentive reader will have noticed that I have used the terms 'afterlife', 'beyond', and 'heaven' (i.e. paradise) interchangeably above. This is no coincidence. It is rather due to the fact that what we know about this realm of departed souls still allows for the coexistence of multiple interpretations. The science of the afterlife remains a dynamic and evolving field, and you will see that not all questions are fully settled. Whether one refers to the place where the dead reside as paradise, heaven, or in more abstract terms, as the beyond or the afterlife depends on one's personal perspective for now, at least in academic circles. Moreover, the early discoveries about the afterlife were compatible with many pre-existing accounts of the other world. In this essay I try to provide a balanced exposition of the most common interpretations and adapt my terminology to the pertinent context.

The discovery of empirical evidence for an afterlife had raised many questions. Can we converse with the residents of that realm? Would we meet our deceased loved ones after death? How do souls in the beyond pass their time? What are the consequences for the living? And, of course, can we contact the Creator? These are all legitimate questions, and I will try to give answers where possible and outline competing interpretations on matters that still await resolution.

The story that has unfolded over the past years is not an easy one to tell. It is especially difficult to take all scientific, social, and theological factors into account, and to keep this text short and accessible at the same time. This is partly due to the fact that no one can really claim to be a dispassionate observer of the events in the recent past. I can only hope that my views approach an objective account.

The beginning of this metaphysical revolution can be traced back to the seminal theoretical research of Professor Alfred Louis Snesenon. What drove this man remains a mystery to this day. Historical research shows that Al (as he was usually called) L. Snesenon had developed a keen interest in the nature of the afterlife early in his life, but little is known about his youth and his early schooling. After he had acquired a degree in theoretical physics from New York University, he proceeded to obtain a doctorate in string theory but was soon bored by his studies, which he considered far too practical. Nevertheless, he finished his dissertation and was offered a position at the Bell Laboratories in New Jersey. There he set out to develop the theory, which eventually opened the door to conversations with the afterlife.

A full exposition of Snesenon's original theory is beyond the scope of this text, because of the highly sophisticated mathematical framework necessary to follow it. However, by now every child knows that Professor Snesenon's work culminated in the so-called quantum soul postulate [1]. This ingenious theoretical work led to the discovery of the quantum soul effect, also known as the Snesenon effect or Snesenon signature [2]. The quantum soul postulate opened the way to measuring signals emanating from souls in the afterlife. I shall not endeavour to describe the physical and information theoretical nature of the Snesenon effect. It suffices to say that the beyond suddenly became a measurable place.

Early on some scientists speculated that the afterlife is a parallel universe or another dimension [3]. Others proposed that the metaverse itself had been discovered [4]. However, these interpretations were the products of highly specialized scholarly discussions. It has to be admitted that Snesenon's ideas were initially met with healthy skepticism. But as I outline below, empirical evidence soon began to accumulate. The entire theoretical edifice was later formalized and canonized as quantum soul theory, also called Snesenology (after its inventor) or faith physics [5]. As the reader is no doubt aware, the latter term has become the standard outside academia. I shall use all these terms interchangeably.

Quantum soul theory postulated that the souls of deceased human beings departed their bodies and soon after reappeared in the afterlife. However, the temporal aspect of the transition was subject to considerable uncertainty. The Snesenon equations did not allow for the calculation of the time differential between death and the arrival in the afterlife as measured in local time in the here and now. How exactly the transition from our mundane universe to that place of eternal bliss occurred was also unclear. Quantum soul theory remains a purely descriptive theory. It works, but no one knows exactly how. When it became clear that the Snesenon effect could be harnessed the first so-called Snesenon engines were built. At the time such a machine filled an entire building.

Professor Snesenon had quickly published early versions of quantum soul theory without much reflection on the possible consequences. A true scientist, he cared deeply about the dissemination of these important ideas under his name only. The knowledge became public before anyone could assess the far-reaching consequences. Soon thereafter Snesenon engines were being built in all countries which could afford the substantial cost of maintaining one. It is for future historians to envision how things would have unfolded had Snesenon's discovery initially stayed a secret.

The first Snesenon engine to ever go online was built in the Bell Laboratories in New Jersey. The resolution of these early engines was very poor, and they had to be handled by large engineering crews. To resolve the differences between individual

Snesenon signatures was (and remains) the biggest technological hurdle in quantum soul theory. Signatures fade in and out of focus. This has led some scholars to propose a sort of soul uncertainty principle, stating that the clearer the signal the shorter the duration of contact would be. As a result, it was difficult to tune those early prototype Snesenon engines to the right settings in order to home in on individual Snesenon signatures in the afterlife. At this point operating a Snesenon engine was more art than science. The first readings were inconclusive. But after long hard work, and substantial government funding, three candidate Snesenon signatures were isolated. For the first time in human history, a team of operators in the Bell Labs was about to establish contact with the departed souls of recently deceased human beings. The genius of Alfred L. Snesenon had enabled humanity to speak to the dead by artificial means.

02

A Better Place

Thinking about these early days, it is difficult not to get excited. The brave men and women working under Professor Snesenon had set out to test the most audacious scientific hypothesis in the history of humankind. Some readers may object that this romanticizing view of historic events is misplaced, given some of the more unsettling revelations about the afterlife we have all come to live with. But we must not judge quantum soul theory by any consequences for our personal lives. Instead we have to appreciate that it opened our eyes to a grander, more magnificent view of the universe. What was about to unfold is nothing short of a true scientific revolution. As a matter of fact, the repercussions far outstrip those of previous scientific revolutions. No sphere of human endeavour remained untouched. Yet, when Snesenon and his team of operators turned on the first Snesenon engine, they could not possibly have foreseen what was about to happen.

After some initial tests promising readings were selected for further inspection. Not all of them turned out to be Snesenon signatures of departed souls, but eventually several candidate signatures could be isolated. One after the other they were to be contacted. Three in particular have to be mentioned in order to understand the early developments of faith physics. These were the souls of Anita Fromm, James Boyle, and Faruk Warsi. Each of their stories will be told in due course. Each served to advance faith physics and theology to new levels. But they have to be mentioned as a group, because their presence in the beyond anticipates most of the key questions in faith physics, some of which even the uninitiated reader may have heard about. From the *common sense paradox* to the *final frontier of faith*, from the search for hell to the *false induction paradox*, the seeds of these highly sophisticated theological concepts were contained in the biographies of these individuals. Nevertheless, we cannot fault Alfred Snesenon and his team for not seeing the inevitable. What seems obvious to us in retrospect was unpredictable for the actors at the time.

But who were these people who had suddenly found a voice? How could it be established that these voices belonged to deceased human beings? The reader may consider these to be ridiculous questions. Nowadays—in our enlightened era of Snesenology—it must appear that way. But back then we lived in a different world: a world of controversy, where the notion of life after death had been disputed by a misguided few. Of course, we now know that this was a nonsensical position to hold, but in the past those pesky individuals demanded empirical evidence or at least logical coherence, fully expecting that neither could ever be delivered. Wasn't life after death beyond the reach of empirical inquiry? Faith physics proved them wrong.

When the operators at the Bell Labs targeted the first Snesenon signature they did not know what to expect. Would there be any sign of intelligence from this thing they were measuring? To everybody's surprise the readings were easily decoded as human speech. The first voice from the beyond belonged to a woman calling herself Anita Fromm, and Anita had a lot to say. However, it must be admitted that her first words constituted a bit of a surprise. Early publications report them as: 'Finally, someone to talk to! They keep ignoring me here.' The operators were perplexed. They? Who? Supposedly other departed souls, academics hypothesized later. The operators tried to question her from the first minute, but she simply ignored them and started telling her life story.

In life Anita had been a nurse in a hospital in rural Africa. Originally born in Austria, she had been raised to be a devout Catholic and had moved to Africa in her early twenties in order to become a missionary. From that moment on she had devoted all her life to help spread the word of God and to protect indigenous people from shamanism, disease, and contraceptives. But Anita's status as a departed soul was still awaiting confirmation. Not everyone was convinced that the first Snesenon engine had indeed established contact with the beyond. The key concepts of faith physics are hard to grasp. Faith physics was a controversial topic at that time and people, including academic scholars, needed convincing.

The first complication to arise was that Anita's body could not be found. It had been well digested by then. Thus the question arose, how one could be sure that the person speaking through the Snesenon engine was not an impostor? At first it was reasoned that Anita's family might be able to confirm her identity, but unfortunately she had no living relatives. It might not have helped anyway. Confirmation by living relatives could not be considered solid evidence. Back then family and friends in the here and now were still eager to believe that their loved ones were in the proverbial 'better place'. Nowadays (as the reader will no doubt be well aware) people are not so eager anymore.

While the Snesenon engine operators struggled to maintain the fragile connection to Anita Fromm's Snesenon signature, they were keen to extract information from her that could in some way verify that she was indeed speaking from the afterlife, or, in fact, from paradise. Apart from the fact that Anita had been a pious Catholic, she had also devoted her life to caring for the sick and poor. Some reasoned that this devotion should have guaranteed her a place in heaven.

I have already mentioned that the distinction between heaven and a generic afterlife has proven to be more difficult than initially imagined. Catholics had high hopes after the first conversations with Anita had been published. After all, the Catholic faith assumed that the departed were reunited with God after death. But even representatives of other faiths showed a lot of interest. Outside of Catholicism, most monotheistic faiths believed that the dead are prejudged after death, with the final judgment to be rendered at the end of times. But even in those faiths the dead do get a taste of what is in store for them, be it good or bad. The implications were intriguing. Could Anita's loneliness hint at the fact that she was in this intermediate state, waiting for the resurrection of the flesh, thus speaking in favour of other faiths? On the other hand, Anita had been a Catholic. Could it be that she had been doing good deeds despite her lifelong belief in what some considered to be the wrong tenets of faith? Of course, this interpretation pointed to Anita experiencing a foretaste of eternal damnation. There was no easy answer to this conundrum. To make matters more complex, for Buddhists and Hindus Anita's state simply meant that she was awaiting reincarnation. But we are getting ahead of ourselves. All these matters will be discussed in greater detail in the following chapters. As a matter of fact, most official representatives of religions other than Catholicism were initially not very enthusiastic about Professor Snesenon's discoveries. They hesitated to proclaim that the existence of heaven had been proven, lest it be misconstrued as an endorsement of Catholicism.

Unable to prove that they were indeed talking to the soul of Anita Fromm, Professor Snesenon and his operator crew decided to simply record everything Anita had to say. Since it is common knowledge by now, even outside academia, you may know that Anita's life story is a tragic one. In her uncontrollable ramblings she told the operators how her broken relationship with her mother and her abusive father had led her to seek a life of solitude and had made her incapable of experiencing sexual intimacy. How she had ended up becoming a nurse and missionary in rural Africa, where she contracted Malaria. How she had experienced sexual violence when civil war had broken out. How she had eventually stepped on a land mine and lost her leg. And finally, how a crocodile had eaten her after she had gotten lost on a recreational visit to a national park. Anita remembered it all. She remembered all the details from her earthly existence right up to those first bites a crocodile took out of her as it pulled her under water. The operators were eager to hear something about the hereafter, but Anita ignored any questions posed to her.

At that time an unpleasant suspicion began to take shape among Snesenon's team. Supposing that Anita was not experiencing a foretaste of eternal damnation: did Anita's account justify the conclusion that other departed souls avoided her company? Researchers on Snesenon's team hypothesized that departed souls should have free will and not live an eternal existence as the Creator's automatons. Was it conceivable that other souls preferred to stay away from Anita? Or were the beatified dead kept in solitary confinement until the final judgment? Since faith physics was not yet widely accepted at the time, this notion could not spark the theological revolution that should have followed. But it was the first bit of information about the afterlife, however uncertain. Anita's state of mind and her solitude were to become the first controversial topic of Snesenology, if only on a small scale.

Meanwhile, Snesenon's team refocused on Anita herself. Prominent psychologists were consulted in the hope to somehow help her come to terms with her situation. She was clearly traumatized. Whatever divine therapy was available in the afterlife, she had not yet benefited from it. This fuelled the developing controversy. Couldn't her memories have simply been erased? Or would that have amounted to some kind of imposed amnesia? Our memories create the reference frame for our individuality. Most people expected that if we were to continue our existence in an afterlife, we would do so with our memories intact. What use would all this earthly toil be if our memories were wiped on arrival in heaven? Before the unstable connection with Anita's Snesenon signature was finally lost, she had been diagnosed with a severe case of post-traumatic stress disorder and clinical depression, with one key difference to earthly equivalents. She was, of course, unable to take her own life. But at least Anita was—it was supposed by some—in a better place now.

Shortly after the connection to Anita had faded, a group of bold cardinals in the Vatican proposed—without the consent of Pope Pious III—a solution to the problems raised by Anita's state of mind. Anita was still waiting to be bathed in supreme glory of the loving Creator. All her mental suffering would soon be substituted by happiness beyond earthly comparison[1]. If this

---

1 The academic terminology 'happiness beyond earthly comparison' refers to the well-defined concept of happiness no living human being can imagine. The reader should not confuse it with the type of happiness we experience in our daily lives, like spending time with loved ones, a sense of achievement, the spiritual high of natural beauty, and so forth.

was indeed heaven, the glory of God should soon erase that pain without erasing her memories. Anita was simply in the 'waiting line', these scholars reasoned. Surely the reader is aware that the notion of the *heavenly waiting line* has always been a key concept in Catholic theology[2].

Notwithstanding such tentative solutions, Anita Fromm's case left many people shaken. But faith physics was a very young discipline at that time. Its validity still had to be established somehow. Unfortunately, Anita had resisted any attempt to extract useful information from her. Doubters intervened, claiming that the so-called conversations with Anita had to be an elaborate hoax. Others held back. So tremendous were the implications of faith physics that, for the time being, even the most zealous believers were hesitant to proclaim that proof for an afterlife had been found. Fortunately, shortly after the connection to Anita's Snesenon signature faded, closing the door to her astral asylum, the next Snesenon signature could be contacted. Only the second connection to date, James Boyle helped elevate quantum soul theory from speculative theory to an established science.

---

2   In these early events, we can already glean an issue which was to plague faith physics and theology from this point onward: the temptation to identify the realm of departed souls with traditional conceptions of heaven or paradise based on the biography of the souls encountered.

03

Finished Business

Shortly after the delicate connection to Anita Fromm had been lost a second Snesenon signature was targeted. Once the conduit to the beyond had stabilized, the soul of James Boyle, formerly a butcher in Arlington, Texas, could be interviewed. However, for several minutes Boyle seemed lost and confused, almost as if he was talking to himself. Tensions were high. Snesenon and his theory were under fire. The operators feared another Anita Fromm debacle. But James Boyle calmed down and started addressing Professor Snesenon and his team directly. He was responsive but unwilling to answer questions. Instead, he asked for his family to be convened with great urgency.

The conversations with Anita Fromm had been released to the public only hours before the incredulous Boyle family was brought to the Bell Labs. Boyle had been a pillar of his local community. A generous man, loved and respected, who had supported many local soup kitchens with his business. But Boyle had been sick for a long time and had eventually disappeared without a trace. His daughters and his brother burst into tears when they heard his voice. For them there could be no doubt that they were speaking to James Boyle. All seemed well until his wife, Erika Boyle, started weeping and withdrew into the corner of the recording chamber where she collapsed. After several long seconds of silence Boyle asked for his family to leave the recording chamber. It soon became clear why. James Boyle accused his widow of having murdered him.

But it was still unclear if Boyle was who he claimed to be. Ever since the first contact with Anita. From it had been a lingering preoccupation of Professor Snesenon and his team that family and friends, left behind after the death of a loved one, were far too eager to believe that the deceased could still be a presence in their lives. Their conviction could hardly serve as the only evidence in favour of faith physics. But by accusing his widow James Boyle had opened up an unanticipated opportunity. Federal agents were rushed to the Bell Labs to interview him. Boyle gave a detailed description of how he was murdered. His wife confessed and confirmed each and every detail of Boyle's description. His body was later found and identified beyond doubt, showing all the indicated traces of the murder and the slow poisoning leading up to it. There could be no doubt. The soul of James Boyle was speaking through the Snesenon engine. The particular circumstances of his murder did not permit any other interpretation.

Nowadays we take the existence of the afterlife for granted, but back then it was difficult for the public to accept these new ideas, especially after the initial shock that followed the public release of the transcripts from the encounter with Anita Fromm. Even while Boyle was being interviewed, people kept offering alternative explanations ranging from alien encounters to deliberate deception. At this time Boyle's Snesenon signature was already fading. After only two cases, researchers did not have enough data to assess the stability of the conduit to the beyond, but in retrospect we can say that James Boyle *stayed online* for an exceptionally long time. Especially given the poor quality (by today's standards) of the Snesenon engine that was used.

Erika Boyle's trial began with considerable media attention. She had retracted her confession. The defence tried to argue that the dead were not to be admitted as witnesses. However, James Boyle was technically not a witness of the prosecution. Irrespective of who had pointed the investigators to the evidence, it remained highly incriminating. Erika Boyle was found guilty and was supposed to be executed under Texan law. Meanwhile contact with James Boyle had become progressively more difficult. Only occasionally his voice would rise above the crackle of static. The Snesenon engine could no longer track his Snesenon signature. But when told about the verdict, he had one last surprise in store for the world. He asked for clemency on behalf of his wife.

The media went wild. The newspaper headlines of those days have been burned into the collective consciousness. They ranged from the emotional 'The dead forgive the living!' to the philosophical 'Should she be convicted if his soul lives on?' Operators tried to reach Boyle one last time, inquiring about his motives. In the last audible recording he simply stated, 'I don't want that bitch up here!' Thus James Boyle, only the second departed soul to ever speak to the living by artificial means, was lost to the beyond again, possibly forever.

Why had Boyle assumed that his murderous widow would join him in the afterlife or heaven? By all accounts Boyle had been a good man. His biography gave further credence to the hypothesis that he should be in heaven or at least experience the foretaste of eternal happiness. Erika Boyle had killed her husband in cold blood. Wasn't she supposed to go to hell after her execution? The answer to this mystery was not forthcoming. By then Snesenon engines were being built around the world.

The proverbial genie was out of the bottle. It was only a matter of time until more Snesenon signatures would be found and more interviews conducted.

The early experiences with Anita Fromm and James Boyle supported the claims made by the proponents of Snesenon's Theory. Commissions were formed to systematically assess the validity of quantum soul theory. The evidence was mounting steadily. But the selection of souls that happened to be found by the early Snesenon engines was rather random. James Boyle was one of the few to stay online for a prolonged period of time. However, the conversations with him had often been tedious, disturbed by constant background noise and static. Boyle had apologized frequently but said that there was nothing he could do. The dead outnumber the living. The afterlife is crowded.

When quantum soul theory gained more and more acceptance people began to ask themselves why Boyle in particular had been contacted. What were the odds that the first souls contacted by the very first Snesenon engine had been victims of violence? In Boyle's case, a murder victim that could point the living to new evidence. It seemed too much of a convenient coincidence. 'Unfinished business' were two words often uttered in the corridors of the Bell Laboratories at the time. Members of the lead engineering team came up with an early theory that tried to explain James Boyle's special circumstances. This was the theory of unfinished business. It posited that Boyle still had things to settle with the living. Was it possible that Boyle's soul was not at rest because of the way he had died? Or rather, the way he had been forced out of earthly existence. In other words, instead of having contacted a departed soul in heaven, could Boyle have been a plain old ghost? The mere thought shocked the proponents of quantum soul theory. They had stated their reputation on the notion that the Snesenon effect allowed for contact with the afterlife. Among others Professor Snesenon distanced himself immediately from these theories. But the issue was not easily settled. By that time Boyle was beyond the reach of Snesenon engines. His signature was lost again. It was conceivable that he had settled his unfinished business and had gone wherever the souls of the dead went once they had resolved all outstanding issues. Unfinished business theory was ultimately disproven when other souls stayed in contact for longer periods of time, souls that had no obvious issues to settle. But the possibility that Boyle and Fromm were ghosts distracted both scholars and laymen from more dramatic implications. No one had yet begun to ask how James Boyle knew where to send the investigators in order to dig up the evidence against his widow.

04

Politics

Unless the reader is familiar with all peculiarities of the history of faith physics, it would only be natural to assume that the first crisis to unfold due to Snesenon's revelations involved theological or philosophical disputes. This was far from the case. While the scientific community was slowly discarding its scepticism and accepting quantum soul theory, the rest of society was still struggling to grasp these novel concepts and their repercussions. However, suspicions were fading. The empirical nature of quantum soul theory began to exert its pull on non-practising believers and people hitherto ambivalent towards religion. This increased the pressure on official representatives of the world's organized faiths to take a positive stance towards faith physics. Nevertheless, the first global crisis affected the political sphere, following the discovery of the soul of Faruk Warsi, the third of the aforementioned key individuals in the history of early faith physics.

When a Snesenon engine (one of the first to be built outside the Bell Labs) homed in on his Snesenon signature, no one could have anticipated the international crises that followed soon thereafter. Before his death Faruk Warsi, a good-natured husband and loving father, had been living in Basra, Iraq. A pious yet practical man, he had little interest in politics and worked as a mechanic. But Faruk's plans to steer clear of trouble and simply keep his family safe were overturned when he overheard two of his customers discussing a planned assassination. Though he had no great love for his political leaders he reported his observation to the authorities, hoping to prevent violence. His trust was not rewarded. Instead the Iraqi secret service and the CIA coerced him into engaging with the terrorists, hoping to uncover the extent and affiliation of the terrorist cell. Through no fault of his own Faruk Warsi had ended up at the heart of a counter-terrorism operation. When unanticipated circumstances arose he had been abandoned and framed as a collaborator. He was eventually captured by the assassins he was supposed to expose and beheaded after several days of torture and questioning. To put it mildly, Warsi was quite unhappy with the way things had turned out for him. Like Anita Fromm he was traumatized and remembered everything. However, unlike Anita Fromm, Warsi was angry and bent on revenge. The connection with him degraded rapidly, but before contact was lost he had revealed as many secrets as he could remember. We cannot be sure how much was censored after his first revelations, but the ruthless use of an innocent man caused a severe diplomatic crisis for the United States and the Iraqi government. More importantly, it suddenly became apparent that, with Snesenon engines being built around the world, countries could do little to stop such secrets from getting out, for Warsi was not alone.

With Snesenon's theory in the public domain, an arms race had begun, a race to build the most capable Snesenon engine. At its core this was a competition among countries to find and contact the souls of deceased spies and diplomats, preferably before other governments did—either in order to interview them about the circumstances of their deaths or to question those of the other side. The collected data would, it was hoped, reveal the ploys behind political assassinations and espionage. But it was all far worse than this scenario suggested. At the time it was not yet clear whether James Boyle's and Anita Fromm's behaviour implied that they were (and still are) able to observe what was happening on Earth while not connected to us through a Snesenon engine. (I will return to this notion further below). It was the foremost question at that time. Intelligence agencies around the world were keen to recruit the dead as unstoppable spies. Curiously only the United States National Security Agency lobbied for a ban on this Ectoplasmic Espionage (EE). It is not clear why, given that EE promised total surveillance of the enemies of the United States.

Men of faith had been remarkably silent during these first months since the invention of the Snesenon engine[3]. But the public pressure in all faith communities mounted steadily. The biography of Faruk Warsi provided another case of a good and innocent man, speaking from the afterlife. Was it not time to finally declare that the Snesenon realm was indeed heaven or some form of pre-heaven? Prompted by the political upheavals and public opinion high standing members of the world's faiths took tentative steps in that direction, stopping short of binding declarations. The issue was raised that if one particular nation was preferred by the Creator of the afterlife—God's own country, so to speak—then this country would enjoy an incredible advantage, since the Almighty could lend a hand in matters of national security. Moreover, with the afterlife all but confirmed beyond any reasonable doubt it was time, they argued, to reconsider the separation of church and state. Surprisingly this

---

3   Catholic scholars are an exception. They had been forced to take a stance when Anita Fromm had been interviewed.

behaviour was mirrored in many nations with differing dominant religions. God seemed to prefer more than one country.

Distrust among nations grew with every departed soul discovered in the afterlife. Snesenon projects had at that point been militarized in many countries, and substantial resources had been allocated to the improvement of early Snesenon engines. Professor Snesenon was highly dismayed by this turn of events and resigned from his post as head of the legendary first operator crew. His invention had taken on a life of its own. International relations were strained. Meanwhile political circles within individual countries had been similarly affected. It was only a matter of time until some dead spy or politician would spill more secrets. Backroom deals, corruption, industrial espionage, personal failings, they were all at risk of being uncovered. Governments began to collapse. Whole cabinets resigned. Older readers may recall that the threat of worldwide chaos was very real at that time. However, in what must rank as the greatest achievement yet in international diplomacy the governments of the world eventually came together in the United Nations and ratified a new international treaty. In this accord they agreed to pass national laws, prohibiting the interviews with Snesenon signatures of deceased politicians, intelligence operatives, bankers and powerful industrialists. Other issues like climate change treaties, nuclear disarmament, or development aid had to be postponed because of this urgent problem. In long and arduous negotiations the political leaders of more than 150 nations agreed to sign the treaty and to enforce it in their countries. We were indeed lucky that the enlightened political class was able to act so swiftly in the interest of the world's population. Of course, it was and still is plausible that most of these individuals in question remain lost in the beyond anyway, among the billions of souls suspected to reside in the afterlife. There was still no way to identify a Snesenon signature prior to contact but our politicians argued that no chances should be taken. Who knows what conflicts could have erupted had they not acted so swiftly?

The implications of early faith physics for global politics are an important topic in itself, which is why I could not neglect it altogether. The role played by Faruk Warsi during these events should not be underestimated. However, this ultimately superficial view obscures far more important implications, which I wish to bring to the reader's attention. Warsi had been a Muslim. James Boyle, on the other hand, had been a Baptist in the here and now. The discovery of Anita Fromm and James Boyle had shocked non-Christians. Similarly, the discovery of Faruk Warsi had now shocked non-Muslims. Something was amiss. Indeed, we find in these early revelations about the afterlife the seed of what was later termed *the common sense paradox*, which we will discuss in great detail in later chapters. Now that faith physics had started to be broadly accepted, people wondered. How could two persons following different religions be found in the same afterlife or heaven? The case of Anita Fromm had given support to the notion that this afterlife was indeed heaven. She had to have been rewarded for all her good deeds, at least according to some scholars. Thus, Warsi's presence in the afterlife not only anticipated the common sense paradox but also the notion of the *final frontier of faith*, two of the largest issues in modern Snesenology. Importantly these discoveries set the stage for the most exciting developments in theology since Thomas Aquinas' proofs of God. However, the time to ask and possibly answer these grand questions had not yet come. But with the international treaty in place, the way was now free for the advancements of military grade Snesenon engines to trickle down to civil society. This sparked a veritable revolution in theology, philosophy, and personal hygiene across the planet.

05

Allegory

The evidence in favour of faith physics had mounted steadily. In a grand gesture, the Nobel committee acknowledged the growing importance of faith physics and created the Nobel Prize for Snesenology. It now complemented the prizes in physics, chemistry, literature, peace, physiology or medicine, and economics, recognizing outstanding scientific achievement. Naturally, Alfred Snesenon was the first recipient. Following the scandalous, if short-lived, militarization of Snesenon projects around the world, the Professor used the prize to establish a new research lab. In a secluded location, he gathered the most promising young minds of the world in order to develop the theory further.

The increasing evidence base for faith physics needs to be contrasted with the more doubtful foundations of the most common interpretations. When it became clear that all departed souls discovered to date seemed to have lived a reasonably pious life (only three of which we have examined in more detail), the number of practising believers surged dramatically all over the world. Suddenly it did not matter any more if official representatives of the world's religions accepted faith physics. The believers had taken the initiative, flooding churches, temples, and mosques. In a fateful decision, leading figures of the great monotheistic religions finally gave up their resistance, implicitly accepting that heaven or possibly the domain where the souls of the departed await the resurrection of the flesh had been found. So great was the benefit of the inflow of new converts that the representatives of different faiths across the world did not emphasize the fact that believers of competing faiths had been found in this afterlife or criticized any explanations offered to that regard. In fact, under the onslaught of a secular Zeitgeist the Abrahamic faiths had already formed a tacit alliance, supporting each other's right to claim that each of them embodied the one true creed. However, in retrospect we can also be fairly certain that the decision to adopt this stance towards faith physics was in part motivated by a fear that reincarnation-based belief systems may gain more traction outside their ancestral homelands. After all, the departed souls could have simply been awaiting reincarnation. Surprisingly, claims of this kind were put forth only at a later stage[4].

The immediate consequences were overwhelming. An intellectual revolution swept across the planet. Agnostics were the first to welcome the irrefutable certainty concerning the afterlife. For so long they had struggled to maintain the courageous and difficult intellectual stance of indifference to any type of rational argument. Now they could almost give themselves to faith. At least some of them, for agnostics now belonged to one of two categories. The first group, calling themselves the *True Agnostics*, welcomed the newly found evidence for an afterlife but did not feel comfortable rejecting

---

4   See Chapter 14.

any other supernatural entities whose non-existence could not be proven, like fairies, elves or unicorns. After all, that there was an afterlife did not tell us anything about the onto-logical status of fairies, elves and unicorns. The second group, the *Fence Sitting Agnostics*, felt that incontrovertible proof of the afterlife clearly restricted the number of possible worlds to one where there was a Creator of the afterlife. By extension his authority governed the laws of possibility[5]. But according to them one still had to be agnostic about all faiths that promised an afterlife. Nonetheless, the revelations of Snesenology did reduce the burden on these agnostics. Take elves for exam-ple. Previously all agnostics (true or not) had reasoned that since one could never definitely prove that elves did not exist, one had to be agnostic about them. Prior to the discoveries of Snesenon, the International Federation of Agnostics (IFA) had painstakingly catalogued all the entities its members had to be agnostic about. From fairies and goblins, through all the gods of humanity's various cultures, to elves, ghosts, the imag-inary friends of little children, the German city of Bielefeld, and many more. At least for the Fence Sitting Agnostics this library could now be reduced to a single tome of only several thousand pages, covering every unknowable aspect of all reli-

---

5   Only marginally different from other natural laws, like the laws of gravity or electromagnetism, the term 'laws of possibility' refers to a concept central to pre-Snesenon agnosticism. If something cannot be refuted, it is in principle considered possible. For instance, even if one has many reasons to believe flying horses do not exist, one cannot commit to their non-existence, since one can never prove a negative statement. This courageous intellectual stance acknowl-edges the possibility—however uncertain—that maybe the next day horses will start flying. The law is valid, not only for traditional supernatural entities like fairies, gods, dragons, and so forth, but, by extension, also for anything that can be imagined; like a moon made of cheese, water not being wet and so forth. The reader may have previously come across the law of possibility although other scholars may have referred to it as the law of imagination.

gions that had incorporated souls and an afterlife into their teachings. This was a great relief for many serious intellectuals and educated laymen who had thus far proclaimed themselves agnostics. They could finally assert with confidence that the tooth fairy did not exist.

However, not everybody welcomed the consequences of quantum soul theory. A group of people for whom Snesenology was truly problematic were the so-called moderate believers. For decades these good-natured people had performed ever more elaborate mental gymnastics in order to accommodate new scientific findings and the changes in social norms in their everyday life while preserving their faith. To many this faith was worth defending because they had worked so hard, usually against the will of their parents and against societal pressures, to acquire said faith (a respectable feat for young children under the age of ten). But the potential problems due to the revelations of quantum soul theory were manifold for these individuals.

Up until this point, the reasoning of these people had been straightforward. If the same scientific theories that gave us medicine, x-rays, electricity and central heating led people to believe that evolution was true, then creation myths had to be allegorical. If the law of nuclear decay gave us the capability to build power plants and smoke detectors, then isotopic age estimates of the Earth and fossils had to be correct too. If the moral Zeitgeist tended to accept homosexuality and condemn slavery, contrary passages from one's favourite holy book had to be conveniently forgotten. If lack of birth control propagated by one's own church spread HIV among the poor, then one had to focus one's mind on the generosity of the local soup kitchen. If the sciences yielded convenient wonders like cars, planes, and Aspirin, then one had to blind oneself to the picture of a vast, indifferent cosmos painted by these very same natural laws. In less enlightened times this could have led to hypocrisy and intellectual doublespeak, but there was a simple and elegant solution: allegory.

Allegory, it is said, conveys hidden messages through symbolic figures, actions, imagery, and events. Moreover, allegory is such a powerful intellectual tool that one wonders why any serious intellectual would try to do without it. It can even adapt to changing circumstances. Before pre-Snesenon science had revealed geological time-scales and Darwin's theory of evolution by natural selection, the vast majority of people had not necessarily viewed creation stories as allegorical. But once new scientific theories had garnered more and more evidence and supporters, the allegorical meaning of creation myths had suddenly become apparent. This is but one example of the truly overwhelming power of allegory. The moment some aspect of Holy Scripture turns out to be factual nonsense it reveals itself as beautiful allegory. This is the awesome explanatory power of allegory.

But even allegory is not without weaknesses. Some aspects of scripture had to be real. All of it could not be allegorical. Otherwise scripture would have been reduced to psychological truths and moralizing stories, like any odd novel. The message in God's words would have been hidden beneath layers and layers of potentially fallible human interpretation. Moreover, there had to have been a moment of genuine revelation, a moment of contact with the Almighty, when the word of God had been delivered for the first time. No! Without some ground truths divine authority is meaningless. How else was one to derive strict instructions about what to do with one's genitals or a set of absolute moral values? However, by discovering irrefutable empirical evidence for the afterlife, Snesenology grounded key bits of faith in reality once and for all. As was famously noted by Alfred Snesenon in his Nobel Prize acceptance speech, faith physics saved allegorical faith from itself.

To be fair, some form of afterlife has probably always been among the few elements of scripture, which have never been called into question by most believers, be they moderate or convinced. After all it had been impossible to disprove, just like the tooth fairy. Nevertheless, the decisive contribution of faith physics has to be recognized. However, this also caused great confusion among the moderates. If the afterlife was a concrete and intangible part of reality, which other elements of scripture were to be taken literally and which allegorically? Faith physics brought this problem of allegorical views of scripture into sharp focus. Previously there had been a simple, straightforward rule. Everything that sounded crazy, offensive, or dumb in the light of modern morals or science was clearly either allegorical or an editorial mistake. Everything else could, at least in principle, be considered literally and historically accurate. But Snesenology had raised the possibility that elements of Holy Scripture, which had previously been considered allegorical, were indeed true.

The reader has to be aware of the impact the discovery of the beyond had on believers now that the findings of faith physics had been largely accepted. At this point everything seemed possible. What about original sin? What about the many colourful stories, which embodied moral teachings? Some more acceptable than other nowadays. This applied to moderate Muslims, Christians, Jews and Hindus alike. Did Allah really split the moon in half? Or was that story allegorical? What then does a split moon stand for? On the other hand, given the possibility of crime-scene-cleaning-miracles (see below) in theory any element of scripture could be non-allegorical. How could it be determined which were and which were not? Clearly the problem needed to be addressed by experts. The only solution was to organize a special series of international theology conferences for the various faiths. Early on during the preparations it became clear that for different faiths with shared elements of scripture (like the flood, life after death, hell etc.), it would have been difficult to reach consensus about which elements were to be considered allegorical and which literal. Nevertheless the first International Congress on Arbitrary Allegory Attribution (ICAAA) began soon after the idea had been put forth.

For brevity's sake I will only report on the Catholic ICAAA. Expert theologians from various universities, interested laymen, and high standing members of the clergy set out to define strict criteria for what could be considered allegorical and what was to be taken literally. It was agreed very early on that the Old Testament should be excluded since—as experts attested—God's word was unintelligible in those texts. This is a lucky coincidence since it would have been hard to find allegorical meaning in obscure shamanic rituals, God-sanctioned genocide, slavery and rape. Why the true meaning of God's word was so difficult to glean in the Old Testament is a matter of on-going debate. An exception is the case of the Ten Commandments. These were to be taken literally. The clear and coherent logic behind this exception is so obvious that I will not dwell on it here. It is generally agreed that given God's infallibility, his infinite love and wisdom, our inability to decipher his message in the Old Testament must be due to our own fault.

Unfortunately, I cannot report the final outcome of these conferences or the strict criteria that were developed there since the debate is still on-going. But interested readers are pointed to the Proceedings of the ICAAA, which spans about 102,339 pages of case studies by now. The ICAAA has become less and less important over the years. However, it can be seen as a precursor of the meetings of the International Society for Snesenology, the Proceedings of which gave rise to the present text.

*****

A note on Crime-Scene-Cleaning-Creator-Miracles

Before we proceed I must briefly explain some academic terminology. By definition, miracles cannot be accounted for by natural laws, psychology, or random coincidences. They have to be performed by the supernatural Creator or its delegates, like saints or angels. After the miracle, the responsibly acting supernatural force re-adjusts all physical consequences of the heavenly intervention in our here and now. Everything. For instance, the energy balance of spacetime, the motion of atoms, and the flow of radiation are neatly put back to normal at the scene of the miracle, just as it had been the split-second before the miracle, in order to fool determinists into thinking nature is predictable. Not unlike a criminal who cleans the scene of the crime after the act, for if clues were left this would provoke unwanted questions. Even worse, in the case of miracles, leaving behind evidence that points to a supernatural cause would leave people with clues (the nature of clues that point to supernatural causes is a hotly debated topic in modern cutting-edge theology). In other words, people would have empirical reasons to believe the miracle, thus undermining the virtue of blind faith. Investigation of

Crime-Scene-Cleaning-Creator-Miracles is still outside the reach of faith physics, but luckily they pose no problem, neither for moderates nor for orthodox believers. Hence we do not need to dwell on miracles here.

06

Euphoria

Although the ICAAA meetings still need to produce their final recommendations on what is and what is not allegorical, at the time it did calm people down to know that experts had taken to solving the problems raised by Snesenon's findings. The conferences sparked the emergence of many similar meetings around the world and ultimately culminated in the formation of the International Society for Snesenology[6]. Universities, churches, and corporations had started to explore the possible uses of Snesenon engines. Contrary to politicians and military personnel, these parts of society were more positive about the possible uses of Snesenon engines once the initial shock had worn off. For some, the scientific confirmation of an afterlife was more than they could have ever hoped for. Only philosophers bemoaned the loss of ontological uncertainty concerning this afterlife. Via quantum soul theory yet another subject had fallen within reach of empirical inquiry, severely limiting the freedom of elegant philosophical theories. But at least funding was finally easier to come by. The philosophy of religion had (and still has) to be rewritten in the light of the exciting findings of faith

---

6   See Chapter 09.

physics. Substantial progress was also expected in moral philosophy given that the dead could be interrogated.

The major religions of the world had by then fully embraced quantum soul theory. Centuries of slow retreat against misguided common sense, the sciences, and plain old logic had made men of faith weary. After the humiliations of heliocentrism, the enlightenment, evolutionary theory, modern astronomy, neuroscience, gay and women's rights, after having had to reform itself to renounce its core texts as partly allegorical rather than literal, after heroic attempts to stay a force for good in the lives of people while constantly losing members of the herd, after all this, organized religion had finally been vindicated. More than that, their supposedly greatest enemy had given them the proof for the existence of an afterlife. The righteous, if underfunded, struggle of about 6 billion believers against the overwhelming power of numbers of about a billion non-believers was finally paying off. Church officials were quick to note that it had all been worth it now. From minor collateral damage like the germ-supported holocaust of Latin America to the Inquisition. It had all been an epic struggle for truth. Now triumph had come. Organized religions could finally rejoice. The matter is, however, more subtle than one would think at first glance.

Following the initial celebration, the implications of the scientific nature of quantum soul theory (and its empirical confirmation) shook the seats of power of the major world faiths. A sudden realization sunk in. In a certain sense, the revelations of quantum soul theory were a blow to faith in its purest and most virtuous form. The empirical evidence for the afterlife, acquired thanks to Snesenon's work, completely and utterly undermined the highest and most glorious virtue of faith—the ability of modern men and women to convince themselves to believe the mythology of Bronze Age goat herders without a shred of empirical evidence. In fact, churches, mosques, and temples around the world found themselves overrun by new converts and it was hard to turn them down after decades of a slow drain of believers in our previous (inappropriately named) ages of enlightenment and modernity.

Two points of view began to develop among men of faith all over the world. One could be termed the pragmatic view. Its proponents suggested that one should not look a gift horse in the mouth and simply accept all these new believers into the flock, even if they had been converted by empirical evidence. Such believers were often called the *empiricist faithful.* On the other side were the *purists,* who claimed that faith physics undermines the true virtue of faith. However, it is suspected that the purists secretly resented the new converts because they had previously lived the high life, eschewing the prescriptions of faith in the absence of evidence. Now the rats were leaving the sinking ship of atheism, agnosticism and vague non-practising belief.

The power struggle between purists and pragmatists did not last long. Concerning the virtues of faith, the pragmatists won in most cases, and the major world faiths relished their return to glory and consideration. This did not sit well with the purists who mockingly called the beliefs of their evidence-based brethren *phaith* instead of faith. Given the gift Professor Snesenon had bestowed on the organized faiths of the world, some Catholics proposed that he should be declared a saint after his death, assuming he would go to heaven. Snesenon himself did not comment on the issue of canonization. He had become increasingly difficult to reach. Rumour had it that he was working feverishly to extend faith physics together with his most gifted student.

Even though debate on canonization was largely hypothetical as long as Alfred Snesenon was alive, it nearly tore the Vatican apart. The rift between pragmatists and purists had just begun to heal when the pragmatists started to argue that Professor Snesenon had done more for faith than any saint ever had. But the purists on the other hand were quick to note that technically Snesenon's work did not stand up to the rigorous criteria for evidence usually required to declare somebody a saint. The key requirement is that there have to be at least two confirmed miracles reported after Snesenon's death, both somehow attributed to him. Though Snesenon technically never performed miracles, some people hailed his theory as being exactly that. Given their earlier defeat, the purists remained rigid concerning this issue. Finally Pope Pius XIII put an end to the controversy by siding with the purists and declaring that upon his death Snesenon would be subject to the same strict criteria for sanctification as previous saints. The issue had to be re-examined after his passing. With official canonization out of the question at the time, an underground movement that worshipped Snesenon began to develop. But its influence has remained negligible.

In retrospect, this infighting has to be seen as a key moment in church history. Superficially it looks as if the purists had regained the upper hand with their victory concerning the canonization of Alfred Snesenon. But many commentators (myself included) believe that Pope Pius XIII had rewarded the pragmatists for their restraint with key positions of power. Only this long-term perspective gives us some insight into how the pragmatists were able to conduct their secret operations surrounding the search for God several years later[7].

The sheer increase in the number of believers based on the influx of the empiricist faithful was also a financial boon for the organized faiths of the world. Nevertheless, this windfall could have been much higher. With irrefutable empirical evidence at their hands, leading men of faith reasoned that they would finally be able to stop investing large amounts of money in enterprises like subsidizing day care for young children. This would have freed up huge investments previously allocated to guarantee the early exposure of

---

7   See Chapter 11.

children to the soothing idea that they are under constant surveillance and may end up being tormented for eternity if they misbehaved. In theory, all the churches would have had to do at this point was wait for the children to grow up and make up their own mind in favour of organized religion in the light of the irrefutable evidence produced by quantum soul theory. Sadly, this hope was ill-founded since any gap left by a retreat from early childhood education could have been filled by alternative (i.e. wrong) religions. Hence the little flock had to be guarded as it always has been.

Proof in the form of conversations with departed loved ones was good enough for the majority of the new converts. However, somewhat surprisingly most of the empiricist faithful converted to the dominant religion of their home country or the religion of their parents. But the mere existence of an afterlife did not necessarily speak in favour of any organized faith in particular, at least not yet. The number of departed souls that had been interviewed was still comparatively small at this time. It remained to be seen who made it into the beyond and who did not. This did not stop the organized faiths from seizing the moment in order to proclaim new teachings, encyclicals and the like. Some of them remain unforgettable to this day. After a long period of intense meditation and study, Pope Pius XIII set out to make his most famous proclamation from the balcony of St. Peter's. In front of a sea of followers, stretching as far as the eye could see, he started his unforgettable speech with the words 'We told you so!' A few months later the Holy See published a book. In ecumenical spirit it had been co-written by the pope and the heads of other major Christian denominations and was entitled 'Guess who's laughing now?' [6]. Finally the pope published what must rate as the most influential papal encyclical of all time, entitled 'Exsuge hic, Richardus Dawkinsus!'[8] [7]. But while the faithful savoured their victory, another part of society plunged into chaos.

---

8   'Suck on this, Richard Dawkins!'

07

The Crisis of Science

Once Snesenology had been firmly established and conferences like the ICAAA had become less of a novelty people began to notice the silence of the scientific community. Alfred Snesenon's discoveries constituted nothing less than a scientific revolution. Academics started to distinguish pre-Snesenon science from post-Snesenon science. Quantum soul physics was hailed as the ultimate triumph of science. A clever hypothesis and the scientific method had produced irrefutable empirical evidence for an afterlife. Why then did so many scientists remain silent? Why had the scientific establishment not been swept along by the wave of euphoria that had electrified the spheres of theology, politics, economics and even the common people?

The simple answer is that traditional or pre-Snesenon science had plunged into a crisis of self-doubt. Before the revelations of Snesenology, approximately 9 out of 10 scientists (at least in the hard sciences) had not believed in an afterlife. The public had mostly not been aware of this. Now these smug atheists and agnostics were struggling with the revelations of quantum soul theory. How was it possible that a considerable portion of the intellectual elite had been led to believe something that was later revealed to be in contradiction with empirical evidence? Had they relied too heavily on the scientific method in their search for knowledge? Could it be that prior to the discoveries of Alfred Snesenon all believers in an afterlife had somehow had access to a source of knowledge that was closed to the minds of the so-called intelligentsia? It is true that Snesenologists had eventually used classical scientific methodology to prove quantum soul theory, but this could not account for the overwhelming majority of people who had always believed in the afterlife, even before Snesenon's revelations. The implications were earth-shattering. Did the faithful successfully use methods hitherto ignored by science?

The crisis of self-doubt turned into an institutional crisis, a crisis of science itself. Pandora's box had been opened. Scientists across the world looked to the faithful in search of other methods they could use. The most obvious unexplored avenue for science was prayer [8], closely followed by revelations [9]. But progress stagnated when a few planes, which were built based on knowledge that had been privately revealed to the construction engineers, fell out of the sky. However, these first setbacks could not discourage the scientific community. After the initial timidity, other novel methods of gathering knowledge were explored. Some of these new methods offered new ways of settling intellectual disputes. Psychology stood out among the sciences as a pioneer in the use of official dogmas, often combined with fatwas against prominent neuroscientists [10]. Still today some neuroscientists require bodyguards in public.

For the publishing companies it was a gold rush. Many new scientific publications sprung up within a very short timeframe. The prestigious Nature Publishing Group launched, among others, *Nature Fatwas* and *Nature Dogma* to accompany the already existing *Nature Snesenology*. Competing publishing companies countered with the *Journal of Comforting Theories* and the sister publication *Journal of Personal Offence*, a journal devoted exclusively to theories that scientists considered personally offensive and thus deemed discredited.

Finally, new methods of gathering knowledge had been tapped. For a while it seemed as if the scientific community had recovered. But a lingering doubt had remained. If pre-Snesenon science had used only a subset of admissible methods, why then had it been so successful? Why did bridges and skyscrapers stand? Why could it be used to build space probes that charted the far reaches of the solar system? Why did modern medicine heal us more often than not? Why did refrigerators and smoke detectors work? It was one of the great pre-Snesenon scientists, Stephen Hawking himself, who tried to find the solution to this mystery. He coined the term 'false induction paradox', for this problem [11] and laboured tirelessly until his death to resolve it. It is one of the great tragedies of our age that so gifted a man squandered his talents thinking about black holes and relativity and only turned to the false induction paradox so late in his life. On his deathbed he is quoted as having communicated through his machines, 'Not seeing the false induction paradox earlier was the greatest blunder of my life.' The paradox remains unresolved to this day. No one knows why the products of pre-Snesenon science work, while the knowledge acquired through the rigorous application of its method erroneously led many people to abandon their belief in an afterlife. The false induction paradox proved to be the beginning of the end. What was once known as the scientific community is shattered today. However, the emergence of post-Snesenon science distracted the public from a critical problem. Only slowly society began to fully grasp the consequences of what we had learned from James Boyle.

08

The Dearly Departed

The decline of traditional pre-Snesenon science marks the end of what scholars generally refer to as early faith physics. It comprises the initial work by Professor Snesenon and the turbulent years in which the first interviews with departed souls were conducted. Professor Snesenon's Nobel Prize and the official recognition of faith physics by the organized religions of the world also fall in this time window. However, at the time Snesenology as a scientific field of study was still in its infancy. It took time to train a first generation of faith physicists and to build the academic structures other disciplines took for granted. Moreover, the small group of practitioners of Snesenology was deeply fragmented. None doubted the empirical basis of the theory, but adherents of different faiths struggled to agree on a common interpretation of the findings at the time. Lacking better explanations, for the time being most organized faiths adopted one of two stances. One, the departed, which had reportedly worshipped other gods, had secretly converted to the correct religion. Two, the interviews with them constituted deceptions by earthly or demonic powers. It was an intellectual crutch, but as outlined above, it allowed the churches, mosques, and temples around the world to concentrate on dealing with the tide of new converts.

The end of early faith physics marks the beginning of a period of chaos. The lack of a coherent intellectual underpinning for the competing interpretations of Snesenology left all players utterly unprepared for what was about to unfold. The darkest hour in the history of faith physics would ultimately culminate in the premature demise of its founder. But it also sparked the beginning of a process which is underway to this day. Snesenology would emerge shaken, but the events I am about to describe also helped shape Snesenology into a fully-fledged academic discipline and lay the groundwork for what scholars refer to as the period of classical faith physics.

While pre-Snesenon science was in decline, the major world religions relished their return to power. Most ordinary people entered a state of bliss. Despite some puzzling revelations by Anita Fromm and James Boyle, the average person was overjoyed by the prospect of eternal life. Their lives as office clerks, stock brokers, or investment bankers finally revealed themselves with absolute certainty as mere preparation for the eternal afterlife. Similarly, many destitute individuals found new hope in the revelations of faith physics. If Scripture was to be believed, a life of poverty, indignity, and pain was a mere prelude to an eternity of divine harmony. Besides, observing all prescriptions of one's favourite holy book often left little time for plotting to overthrow your oppressors.

Thanks to previous military spending, smaller, more affordable Snesenon engines were coming to market. With progress came miniaturization. The cost of these engines was still prohibitive for the vast majority, partly due to the necessary filters required by the governments of the world. But they were within reach of a select few. Based on Alfred Snesenon's most recent work, ingenious engineers had also improved the resolution of the Snesenon engine. It had become much easier to pinpoint the Snesenon signatures of specific individuals in the afterlife, but only if they were recently deceased. The prospects were intriguing. However, no one had yet fully appreciated the implications of James Boyle's revelations concerning the evidence against his widow.

In earlier times, before the advent of Snesenology, people had often looked to the sky, especially after some heartfelt loss, telling themselves that a deceased loved one was not really gone and that he or she would watch over them. Some people had always believed it. Some used to say so to console themselves. Unknowingly these people had been right all along. Those who had access to the first household Snesenon equipment soon discovered that their loved ones were indeed watching over them. What this really meant had not been clear at that time, but in retrospect James Boyle's behaviour had been full of hints.

It all started with the case of Felipe Gonzales. A cheerful young boy with a strong sense of justice, he grew up to study law. He had always had a strong relationship with his beloved grandparents and had been deeply affected by their recent death. His well-endowed family was among the first to buy a household Snesenon engine. The Gonzales Family used their engine almost every evening to try to converse with recently deceased family members or celebrities. These early models were still difficult to operate, and connections were established only on rare occasions.

Seemingly unrelated Felipe begun to exhibit severe mood swings. After two years of diligent work at university, his academic performance had dropped sharply. Things seemed to improve when he started seeing a psychologist, although Felipe was not very forthcoming in his therapy sessions. To the wider public Snesenology was still a novelty, and his psychologist did not connect Felipe's state of mind to the Snesenon engine Felipe's parents had recently acquired. After Felipe hanged himself unexpectedly, his suicide note brought clarity. At the time of his death he could not bear the shame anymore. Apparently his grandparents had caught him masturbating daily. 'Caught him' is, of course, not the right expression. It turned out that his grandparents had had a constant watchful eye on their grandson and would scold him every time a connection via the Snesenon engine was established. All his failings would come up in these talks. The humiliation must have been unbearable, knowing that he had been watched in his most intimate moments. Shame, anger, and a profound feeling of helplessness eventually led him to suicide. When the grieving family publicized the case it finally dawned on people what it really meant for the dead to watch over them.

The early political crises had involved the departed sharing secrets acquired during their own lifetime. But this was different. It became clear that early suspicions were indeed justified. The departed could observe the living from the afterlife. They did indeed watch over us. The corporate and political spheres were shaken, again. Lawmakers were at a loss. In an act of desperation many countries passed some variation of the American 'limits to supernatural freedom act'. But this law could hardly be enforced. For the overwhelming majority of people the law changed very little. Most were now terrorized by the idea that dead friends, family members, and co-workers might indeed be watching over them in their most private moments. Every little weakness, every personal failing, every written word, had potentially been witnessed by the all-seeing eyes of the dead. The organized faiths of the world were utterly unprepared for this. Their half-hearted interpretations of faith physics had focused on accounting for the fact that believers of competing religions had apparently made it into the afterlife. Now they were all hit equally.

The revelation that the dead were indeed watching over us had a multitude of consequences. For some of the empiricist faithful, the issue was enough to warrant a retreat from their newly acquired convictions. For the first time since Alfred Snesenon's original discovery, the number of believers began to decrease the world over. Many people voiced their anger in worldwide, violent protests. Gathering in large public squares with banners facing toward the sky, they were chanting slogans like 'Stop watching over us!', 'No more spying on the living!', or 'Get your pornography elsewhere!' For others the heavenly overseers were the ultimate expression of God's well-meaning supervision. Theologians proposed that allowing the dead to spy on the living had to be one of the arrows in God's quiver of justified divine punishment[9] [12]. Other scholars suggested that this was indeed how God maintained a record of our conduct in the here and now [13]; via a vast bureaucracy in the sky, aided by an army of informers that never tires, never sleeps. Not unlike a totalitarian surveillance state, only in a good way, of course[10]. Some academics preferred the more elegant and simple explanation that God works in mysterious ways. There had to be some deeper meaning in this affair. Others advocated for the free will of souls in the afterlife. Not everyone considers the matter settled. In fact, towards the end of this introduction I will propose a novel, revolutionary solution, which may resolve this and other outstanding problems of contemporary faith physics.

There can be no doubt that the chaos which ensued after these striking revelations about the departed was a prerequisite for the

---

9   Buddhist and Hindu scholars, though still largely absent from the public discussion, took a more pragmatic stance. Since all the departed would be reincarnated sooner or later and forget their previous existence, one could simply not care about this constant surveillance.

10   The reader may be tempted to suggest that this solution would somehow imply that the Creator is not omnipotent. This would be a fallacy. The simple act of delegating work to the departed does not warrant the conclusion that God could not perform the task himself if he were inclined to do so.

coming together of scholars from various fields of study and from different creeds, which will be the topic of subsequent chapters.

Irrespective of the reasons behind this state of affairs, the consequences were far-reaching. The most striking change in behaviour at a global level occurred in attitudes towards nudity and sex. Younger readers may be puzzled by this terror. These readers have, of course, grown up with all the typical coping strategies people subsequently adopted. But we need to be aware that at the time of discovery this situation led to drastic changes for the entire world population. People started undressing only under cover of complete darkness. As you may or may not know first hand, sexual intercourse is now also practised exclusively in the dark or has been abandoned altogether. For most this also included forgoing masturbation. This was welcomed by the major faiths of the world, especially by Christians. Heaven's supervision finally helped to enforce the prohibition of masturbation. The one positive aspect of the whole matter was that the rate of new HIV infections dropped dramatically. Pope Pius III was quick to note, 'Abstinence does work!' But the lack of masturbation also had the unfortunate side effect of a general rise in stress levels, the sale of antidepressants, number of divorces, teenage suicides, office shootings, and the general crime rate. In addition, the birth rate plummeted the world over. Alarmists saw human civilization in danger. While people could stop having sex, they could not stop showering and defecating. This is why we carry out these activities mostly in total darkness nowadays, hoping that the dead are not able to observe if they were so inclined. This also led to an unfortunate increase in the number of deaths by slippage in the tub. I will not discuss the more dire consequences for personal hygiene in this treatise. In some Muslim countries the heavenly spy scandal led to the burka being mandatory even in the home. Women could otherwise not be shielded from the eyes of departed souls. It was only possible to remove it for the occasional act of procreation in total darkness.

However, contrary to what the reader might think at this point, being watched was not the biggest problem for society. In hospitals terminal care units everywhere shut down, and research into cures for deadly diseases largely ceased or was replaced by research into pain alleviating compounds. Now that everybody knew there is an afterlife, people began to reason: what is the point? The only remaining concern was to die comfortably. Death was now like a relocation to a far away country where everyone would be united with his or her loved ones. Whether or not one would like to be united with former loved ones after death was a different matter altogether. Only a small minority of people cautioned against this, possibly premature, lack of enthusiasm for life on Earth. Given the fact that the dead were not forthcoming about their (for lack of a better word) *living conditions*, they argued we should still try to extend life in the here and now. Maybe life was not so bad after all. No one knew what the departed souls did all day long. Could they meet each other? Were there limits to their freedom? Were they consuming nutrition? The increasingly intense discussion of these and other questions was only the beginning. The issue of the heavenly spies became the catalyst for the formation of a professional faith physics research community, that would tackle the outstanding questions in Snesenology in a more systematic manner. Out of the chaos grew what we call classical faith physics today.

09

Silence

As I have hinted at above, the shock of the most recent discoveries was a catalyst for a more systematic approach to the problems of Snesenology. And for a short while it was mostly unfettered by differences of creed. Scholars also finally turned their attention to God *himself*, the Creator and supposedly the managing director of the afterlife (I follow the convention of referring to God as male, but God's gender is a subject of on-going heated debate). If there is an afterlife, there should be a god, most people reasoned. It may seem odd to the reader that this question was being tackled only now, but one had to live through those early, chaotic years to appreciate the impact of Snesenology. Societies across the world were in shock following Professor Snesenon's work. During the early developments of Snesenology, the technology had been in the hands of a select few. When the initial shock had worn off and Snesenon engines became more widely available, the (still on-going) issue of the heavenly overseers grabbed everybody's attention. It is hardly surprising that a systematic inquiry into the nature of God and the afterlife took a back seat to more immediate concerns.

This is not to say that the age-old questions about the Creator did not play on everybody's mind. Sooner or later a systematic inquiry had to begin. However, the departed seemed quite unwilling to reveal anything about the afterlife. When questioned about the Creator, the answers ranged from 'I don't know' or 'I can't tell you' to the ever popular 'You would not understand' or 'His ways truly are mysterious.' Laymen, clergy and scholars were coming up against a brick wall. After the initial euphoria the afterlife suddenly seemed more trouble than it was worth. With the political and social impact of the dead watching over their loved ones (and others), it was believed that enduring these unpleasant surprises would at least be rewarded with answers to the ultimate questions about life, the universe and everything. Who but God would be able to give satisfactory answers?

The cryptic replies provided by departed souls angered many people, including high standing members of the world's major faiths. Was this not the opportunity to settle once and for all which of the roughly 10,000 religions in earth's history this afterlife belonged to? Which religion had got it right all along? Why did God not reveal himself and declare which among all the competing metaphysical and moral claims were the correct ones? Ordinary people were not aware of the strain this had placed on men of faith until Pope Pius XIII famously became the third Pope to resign from his God-appointed position in order to devote his life to pottery and building World War II model planes.

It was also long rumoured that Professor Snesenon was guilt-ridden and blamed himself for the unfortunate state of affairs. Once it had become clear that nothing could be done against the constant watchful eyes of the dead, many people started to change their everyday habits. But not everybody adapted easily. It is said that Professor Snesenon is the only person in the history of humanity to have received hate mail and death threats in all the spoken languages of the world. It must have been too much to bear. His life's work had essentially plunged the world into chaos and then into despair. Professor Snesenon's suicide was celebrated in the streets once it was made public. Interestingly, his Snesenon signature has not yet been located.

On one level it is understandable that public opinion turned against him. Nevertheless, it is tragic that such a brilliant man was driven to suicide. However, we are fortunate that his star pupil is carrying on his research, honouring Snesenon's legacy. As we will see in later chapters, this work may ultimately give us the answers to all outstanding questions in faith physics. But before we can delve into these fascinating, advanced aspects of Snesenology, we must first recount other key episodes from the history of faith physics, in order to get a more nuanced and complete view of how the field developed.

In tandem with the recent revelations about the departed, Snesenon's death, a mere eight years after his monumental discovery, renewed the determination of many Snesenologists, theologians, and men of faith. The status quo was unacceptable. The big questions had to be addressed. It was at this moment in time (in the year 2030) that—inspired by the success of the ICAAA congress—interested laymen and experts on Snesenology came together to found the International Society for Snesenology. The Society organized an international meeting under the same name (ISS). This annual meeting was the largest among a multitude of similar conferences. The acronym ISS, previously used for the International Space Station, was adopted without complaints from space agencies around the world since no one cared about space any more. Once the afterlife had become a confirmed scientific fact it became completely irrelevant that the Earth circled a regular, unremarkable star in an unremarkable galaxy, which was one among billions in an unimaginably old cosmos. Even so, it is puzzling why God has created that infinity of space when the most important part of existence (eternity) was spent in the afterlife and the second most important part exclusively on Earth.

Incidentally, this is exactly the type of question for which the ISS meetings provide a forum. The long-term goal of the ISS remains to find answers to profound, conceptual problems. Initially theologians and Snesenologists focused on more specific topics. At the early ISS conferences scholars gave talks or presented papers with intriguing titles such as 'Why does God not speak to us directly?', 'What are the dead hiding from us?' or 'What do they do all day?' Some specialists asked: 'Why can schizophrenics and epileptics perceive the voices of the dead without a Snesenon-engine?' (I will discuss mental disorders in more detail below). 'Do the dead eat?' was (and still is) a popular topic even among laymen. Many philosophers and psychologists stated that consumption of delicious food was among the genuine pleasures of life. But if they ate, did the souls of the departed have to digest their food? Worse, did they defecate? What then were the sanitary conditions in heaven? Some scholars proposed that partially digested food would be transmuted into benign, odourless gases by the Creator [14]. In this sophisticated vision of the afterlife, the chief obsession of the Creator was to constantly pay attention to the bowels of departed souls in order not to spoil heaven. Some thinkers took a more pragmatic and plausible stance and proposed that soul excrement simply did not stink, greatly reducing the burden on the Creator [15]. The nature of heavenly excrement became the dominant obsession of theology for a while.

The many subfields of Snesenology and different faiths were, of course, interested in different aspects of the God-question. Thus these big conferences were usually accompanied by smaller satellite workshops for special interest groups, addressing questions like 'Why don't they care about the promised land?', 'Can you finally tell us who should stay in Jerusalem?', and 'Why does eating pork not ban you from heaven?', or 'Who are the virgins?' The latter question aroused special interest and controversy even outside academia. The participants discussed for instance how the Creator assured that there were exactly 72*N virgins for N martyrs [16]. A related question was whether the 72 virgins promised to martyrs were other departed souls or not. An affirmative answer would imply that some virgins probably still have living relatives. How could the Creator design an afterlife where dead virgins (one would think that this was punishment enough) were given to some martyr? Needless to say, this eternal, divinely sanctioned rape aroused the anger of people who had lost loved ones who were suspected of having died a virgin (mostly mathematicians, engineers, and computer scientists). But worse than this, after 72 sexual encounters the martyrs would run out of virgins. On top of this, an eternal afterlife implied an infinity of time. Simple calculus tells us that 72 virgins for an infinity of time tends towards zero, thus implying that martyrs are rewarded with celibacy. So God apparently had to constantly 'revirginise' those poor virgins or alternatively supply fresh ones (increasing the mathematical complexity of the problem) to keep the number at 72. Did the Creator really monitor the virginity of the women given to martyrs? In response to this some Islamic scholars proposed that the virgins might be newly fashioned by God and preserve eternal virginity through multiple sexual encounters. The annals of the science of Snesenology are filled with sophisticated back and forth arguments among accomplished theologians for and against continued revirginisation. Ideally the reader will be able to follow the logic in such scholarly articles, once he or she has finished reading this introductory text.

10

Questions

Despite the success of the early ISS meetings, it soon became clear that the faith physics community was fragmenting. Too many scholars worked on disparate questions. Most commentators believe that the international faith physics community had grown too quickly. There was too little crosstalk between the subfields. This made it difficult for practitioners to come up with grand, all-encompassing theories. In fact, no one had yet dared to tackle the biggest of all questions directly. No one had yet considered how we could learn more about the Almighty himself, apart from through interviews with the departed.

It came as a shock to most Snesenologists and laymen alike when an intrepid group of Snesenon engineers from the Bell Laboratories promised the impossible. They announced nothing less than that they had figured out how to use the Snesenon effect to talk to the Creator himself. Some of them had worked under Alfred Snesenon until he founded his new lab. They resigned from their prestigious posts and formed a start-up company, claiming to have designed a new type of Snesenon engine. But to build a single machine of this new type required a huge investment. At first they tried to attract venture capital.

But a financial return on such an investment was highly improbable. The organized religions of the world were also reluctant to fund the project since its outcome was uncertain at best. Representatives argued that such an investment would divert too many funds from humanitarian projects, such as selling conversations with the departed to individuals that could not afford their own engine.

In order to raise the necessary funds, the engineering team decided in favour of a funding campaign on the Internet. The media went wild. Interested individuals could pledge any amount of money to support the project. In exchange they were allowed to submit a question for God, in case the project was successful. Contributions were ranked according to the amount of money pledged. The higher the contribution the higher up in line one was to ask the first question. The funding run was an overwhelming success. All over the world people gave what they could, but especially rich individuals had been very generous. These substantial contributions had not been anticipated. It is astounding that these individuals parted with large amounts of money in order to ask God a question, given that their lives are so much fuller of meaning and joy than those of ordinary people. The response to the project was so overwhelming that the engineering team even tried to caution its own supporters. After all, there was no guarantee that the modifications to the standard Snesenon equations and the resulting engine would actually work as intended. Contact with the Almighty was still an uncertain prospect at best. But at that point the project had grabbed the world's attention. Nobody wanted to hear words of caution.

The financial might of specific individuals was bound to create resentment. Due to them poorer individuals were pushed towards the end of the queue. An online subculture developed around the project with less well-endowed supporters mocking rich backers, joking that God would slap the rich in the face if they asked too mundane a question. Some high profile backers of the project actually retracted their commitments (legal battles are still on-going) because finding a suitable question to ask the Creator of all things was a daunting task. But not everybody was as fearful. Anonymous statistics of the top questions (dominated by the large number of low-income supporters) showed that many people shared a more pragmatic approach. The second most asked question was if the Almighty had ever tried to create the fabled stone that was so heavy that even he himself could not lift it. Closely followed by the ever popular 'If you made everything, who made you?' A surprising fourth was whether he would reveal the lottery numbers for some future date. Number five was a collection of pleas to help a particular sports team to win, closely followed by the appeal to end world hunger. Another popular choice was 'How come you are so clear about which part of our genitals we should cut off but then work in mysterious ways when tsunamis hit, women are raped with rifles, and children step on land mines?' And, of course, oil money from the Gulf bought enough questions to try to resolve the 72 virgins issue once and for all. However, the most popular question by far was why the Creator allowed the departed souls to spy on the living. Why would he not stop them from watching over us?

Supporters of the project fell into various camps. Young-Earth creationists and theists were easily discernible according to their stance on evolution. Representative questions were, for instance, 'Did you put dinosaurs in stones to test our faith or is the devil trying to fool us?' (technically two questions), or 'Why did you make hundreds of billions of Galaxies with hundreds of billions of stars each in the last 6000 years

79

if everything important is happening on Earth?' Interventionists, on the other hand, were equally easy to recognize based on questions like 'Why did you guide evolution to produce brains that are so easily manipulated to induce out of body experiences and visions of a light at the end of a tunnel?' Theists posed—it has to be admitted—the most tedious questions, like 'Why did you create the world if you already knew how it would turn out?'

Once the funding was secure and the questions catalogued, the engineering team went to work. The new Snesenon engine could finally be built. It was modified in such a way that the team could scan the parallel heavenly universe in broad sweeps, rather than homing in on localized Snesenon signatures. The team hypothesized that in this way they might finally be able to pick up a signal that would rise above the background noise, hoping it would carry messages from the Creator himself. Responding in the same manner would then open up a two-way communication channel. Initial experiments yielded little success. Many of the backers grew less patient by the day. Then suddenly, late one night, crackles of static were picked up. The tension in the control room must have been unbearable. Were they about to hear the voice of God? Could it be that these intrepid engineers would be the first to talk directly to the Creator of all that was and ever will be? Accounts of what exactly happened that night differ, but the end result is the same in all of them. Apparently a sequence of 42 beeps was heard, with some people arguing that God had just spoken in Morse code. Unfortunately, the sequence made no sense in any Morse alphabet. Fringe groups still claim that some higher power had indeed communicated with us, but most Snesenologists believe that it must have been some sort of interference generated from the averaged Snesenon signatures of the billions of souls that must inhabit the afterlife. No coherent signal was ever picked up again, and the start-up is still engaged in a legal battle with its supporters. The time for questioning God had not come. Not yet.

11

Punishments

Several years after the founding of the ISS, following the first attempt at contacting the Creator, it became clear that classical Snesenology was on the brink of a crisis. But the failed attempt to contact God had attracted a lot of attention, especially from Christians and Muslims. The company that had tried to contact the Almighty had eventually filed for bankruptcy. While it was unknown at the time, it is by now common knowledge that key members of that legendary engineering team had been recruited by rogue elements in the secret service of the Vatican—not unlike the Nazi engineers who had been brought to America to kick-start the U.S. space program after World War II. According to rumours at the time the Holy See offered to settle any financial liabilities in exchange for the expertise of the core engineering crew. The team was recruited for a special project in the Holy See. Today we know that the purpose of this secret project was to determine if the Catholic version of hell was sufficiently cruel and frightening.

This motivation may come as a surprise to the reader. The issue has not yet been discussed much outside of scholarly circles. You may wonder: was this really necessary? Surely the concept of hell had been very efficient in causing irreparable psychological scaring to the minds of countless children? It could have been considered proof that many of them matured to be properly dysfunctional adults. But that was not good enough. Radical elements in the Holy See wanted to make sure that it was the cruellest version of hell imaginable. Today we know that the leading members of this rogue group belonged to the pragmatist faction in the Vatican and that they had a hidden agenda. The reasons for this endeavour will become clear in a moment. To understand why exactly data on hell had to be collected we need to remind ourselves of Pascal's Wager.

Pascal's Wager refers to an idea proposed by the 17th century French philosopher, mathematician, and physicist Blaise Pascal. It goes something like this: in the absence of evidence for or against the existence of God there are four options. First, God exists, but one happens not to believe in him. Second, he exists and one does believe in him. Third, he does not exist and one does not believe in his existence. And finally, he does not exist, but one believes in his existence nonetheless. Given that the loving Creator had envisioned the supreme punishment of eternity in hell, according to Pascal one should assume God's existence, just in case, and then follow the given tenets of the faith. In the event that God does not exist no harm is done, it was reasoned. The worst that can happen in this case is that one follows the benign and well-intentioned prescriptions of an unjustified faith. But in the best-case scenario, i.e. if one justly believes in God's existence, one is assured eternal life and happiness and, more importantly, one is spared from hell.

While Pascal's Wager was always a popular rhetorical device, deep down there was a problem. One had to assume the existence of one particular God, ultimately making the wager a circular argument. It was possible to follow the same logic concerning another deity. For example: first, the Mayan Death Gods exist, but one happens not to believe in them. Second, they exist and one does believe in them. Third, the Mayan Death Gods do not exist and one does not believe in their existence. And finally, they do not exist, but one believes in their existence nonetheless. Given that the Mayan Death Gods torment evildoers in the underworld (Metnal or Xibalba), according to Pascal, one should assume their existence, just in case, and then follow the given tenets of the Mayan religion. In the event that those deities do not exist no harm is done, Pascal's Wager suggests. The worst that can happen in this case is that one follows the benign and well-intentioned prescriptions of an unjustified faith.

The argument is so powerful that it actually applies to any faith that includes rewards and punishments. For instance, first, the Fire-Breathing Purple Chicken of Cyprus exists, but one happens not to believe in it. Second, the Fire-Breathing Purple Chicken of Cyprus exists and one does believe in it. Third, the Fire-Breathing Purple Chicken of Cyprus does not exist and one does not believe in its existence. Finally, the Fire-Breathing Purple Chicken of Cyprus does not exist, but one believes in its existence nonetheless. Given the supreme punishment envisioned by the Fire-Breathing Purple Chicken of Cyprus (it pecks with its fiery beak at your genitals for eternity) one should, according to Pascal's Wager, assume the existence of the Fire-Breathing Purple Chicken of Cyprus, just in case, and follow the given tenets of faith[11]. The worst that can happen in this case is that one follows the benign and well-intentioned

---

11   The reader may not be familiar with the religion of the Fire-Breathing Purple Chicken of Cyprus. This is hardly a surprise since it is only practised by a vocal minority of yak herders living on the Kazakh steppes. Curiously it is not believed to have originated in Cyprus. The name is somewhat of a mystery. But whoever is born into the faith of the Fire-Breathing Purple Chicken of Cyprus believes that the chicken has bestowed upon humanity a set of absolute moral values, which must be followed. Otherwise eternal damnation awaits. I am told their hymns and prayer songs are of such great beauty to make even the most staunch critic cry, which of course means that they must contain truth.

prescriptions of an unjustified faith. Crucially, belief in Pascal's Christian God, belief in the Mayan Death Gods, and belief in the Fire-Breathing Purple Chicken of Cyprus are all mutually exclusive[12]. Hence there is no way to decide between the three. In fact, there was no way to decide between any of the roughly 10,000 religions of humanity. That is, prior to faith physics.

Snesenology points us once more in the right direction. Before the advent of faith physics, the only sensible conclusion to draw from all this was to assess the risks (i.e. comparing the promised rewards and punishments) associated with each of the roughly 10,000 religions that either have existed or still exist on Earth and to choose to follow the one religion that promised the most severe punishments, hence avoiding at least said punishments[13]. In the arms race of punishments, Christianity and Islam had been the top contenders with their intricate and sophisticated versions of eternal damnation and hellfire.

This is where the secret project of the Vatican enters the equation. The publicly funded, modified Snesenon engine had failed to contact God. But the leaders of the rogue secret service cell in the Holy See had hoped that the new Snesenon engine might at least be used to find hell by searching for inverse Snesenon signatures (a highly speculative concept proposed by Professor Snesenon in his last published paper). The aim was to collect data on hell. The reason for this was simple. The acquired knowledge about hell could have been used to convince more of the empiricist faithful who were currently worshipping false gods. With knowledge of the types of punishments experienced in hell, the Vatican could

---

12   We will discuss further implication of this mutual exclusivity in great detail in later chapters.

13   Indeed this is what most educated believers did before the advent of Snesenology.

have kept that knowledge secret and call for a new Vatican Council, which would have promulgated an updated vision of the nature of hell. The plans for the modified Snesenon engine would have been leaked to the press several years later. Independent Snesenologists around the world would have built the new engine and confirmed the Catholic version of hell in each and every detail. The pragmatists that had formed the rogue cell in the Vatican's secret service had reasoned that this new empirical evidence would have had an equally strong effect as the initial discovery of the afterlife. It was an ingenious plan. The discovery of the afterlife had compelled doubters to accept the reality of an afterlife, but almost all of them had converted to the dominant religion of their home country. This time the evidence would have swayed the balance of power among the world's faiths in favour of Catholicism. The beautiful logic behind Pascal's Wager would have compelled most of the empiricist faithful to choose Catholicism as their religion, because the only sensible conclusion to be drawn from the Wager's inability to differentiate between religions is to worship the cruellest god.

However, the project was discovered because of the high energy consumption of the modified Snesenon engine once it had reached an early testing stage. The Vatican was thus forced to abandon the project. It had been a proper conspiracy within the Holy See, but to its credit, it was not only uncovered but also fully disclosed. The conspirators were quickly excommunicated, but the new pope and leading cardinals were never able to shake off the lingering doubt in public perception that this project had been sanctioned by members of the clergy at the highest level. On the other hand, unnamed sources in the Church were reported to have said that the question of hell might better be left unsettled, lest—just like the afterlife—hell turned out so different from its previously imagined state that it would have required too stark a change in official doctrine.

12

Criminals

With hell inaccessible, laymen and experts alike were once again captivated by other problems. First among these was still the silent God. It seemed as if all approaches were doomed to fail—almost as if the Almighty himself did not want to be found. Theologians around the world tried to develop new theories which allowed for the inclusion of such a deity. But the truth is that faith physics was at a crossroads. After the disclosure of the Vatican's secret project, the tacit agreement among men of faith not to monopolize the afterlife finally began to crumble. But there was—despite the monumental discoveries of faith physics—still no way to determine which of Earth's religions was correct.

While people were still grappling with the implications of the silent God and the constant heavenly surveillance, the balance of powerlessness among the religions was briefly disturbed. A peculiar finding allowed one particular faith to lay claim to the afterlife for a short while. Some time after the failed attempts to contact God the curious and scandalous case of Heinrich Donton, a German immigrant to the American state of Virginia, led to a shocking revelation. It is not really known what had driven him, but Donton had killed his wife and three bystanders in cold blood. His aged parents later testified that Heinrich had been a troubled man all his life. His trial went by largely unnoticed, for at the time he was not yet at the centre of public attention. Donton was convicted of murder. The governor of Virginia went ahead and signed off on his execution.

During Donton's trial nobody had made the effort to find his wife in the afterlife. To contact the dead in every court case was still economically unfeasible practice. Even if somebody had offered to cover the cost there would have been no guarantee of quickly locating her Snesenon signature. This was not surprising. The dead far outnumber the living. Even with the most up to date Snesenon equipment homing in on the Snesenon signature of any one particular soul was very improbable, time consuming and not always guaranteed to succeed. From the very beginnings of quantum soul theory, the time course of the transition from the here and now into the afterlife had never been quantifiable.

While no one was surprised that, given the limits of Snesenon engines, it was difficult to find Mrs Donton in the afterlife, it came as a shock when a Snesenon engine operator in Russia established contact with Heinrich Donton's soul. Donton expressed deep regrets about what he had done. Further conversations with him were not particularly revealing, but the mere fact that his soul had been found was shocking. How could a convicted murderer reach the afterlife? The silent God was a mystery. A murderer in heaven was a contradiction and a scandal.

From this moment onwards it gradually became clear that not all souls had been innocent in life. Some had even been, like Donton, known criminals. In common language: bad people had made it into what was thought to be heaven. The possibly premature attribution of the status of paradise or pre-heaven to the Snesenon-Realm had always been problematic. Now the pressure mounted even further. In the second wave of global apostasy some of the empiricist faithful left their respective religions. Why were the souls of murderers, child molesters, drug lords, and war criminals to be found in this afterlife? The issue became an existential problem for most faiths[14]. But for one particular faith it was a huge opportunity. Could it be that this was evidence in favour of the Protestant faith?

Not all Protestants agreed, but American Protestants in particular were quick to claim metaphysical victory. For some of them the presence of criminals in the afterlife clearly pointed towards Protestantism. Contrary to Catholics, Protestants did not require a mediator in the form of a priest in order to converse with their God. Protestants could achieve absolution not exclusively through a priest, but through a personal relationship with God. Thus the fact that murderers, rapists, and war criminals were present in this afterlife was taken up by Protestant churches as evidence that their faith was the only true one. After all, even a last minute plea for forgiveness, a silent, internal conversion while strapped to an electric chair, was acceptable, as long as it was genuine. Repent and you will be saved. God forgives all.

This caused quite an uproar, and for some time Protestants were excluded from ISS conferences. Some Protestants even went as far as to suggest that all of the souls so far discovered were indeed Protestants. It was slightly unlikely, but at least in theory it was possible that all those individuals contacted thus far had converted to Protestantism in the last seconds of their life. Especially in cases like Faruk Warsi's this did seem a bit farfetched, but for a

---

14   Again, religions that did not require the notion of paradise were an exception. Faiths that posited reincarnation were immune to these problems. The criminals would simply be reborn as flies, frogs, or toilet brushes. In fact some of the empiricist faithful switched their allegiance to these faiths. With the fragile truce between competing faiths broken, it was only a matter of time until this argument was to be put forth.

while it was the only sensible theory that fitted the data. Indirect support came from the fact that the departed souls did not really speak about their own religion. Needless to say, other faiths did not accept this interpretation.

This state persisted for little more than a year. Things only calmed down when better and cheaper Snesenon engines became available. With a lower price and increased resolution, the number of contacted souls skyrocketed. The cost had finally reached a level where the citizens of emerging economies could afford their own household Snesenon engines. When a number of departed souls of Chinese nationals was found in the after-life, the Protestant victory dance stopped abruptly. It was highly unlikely that the rising number of Chinese souls had all converted to Protestantism in the last moments of their lives. Of course, the roughly one billion Chinese were not in the least bothered by this. They had always cultivated a vague form of belief in their ancestors without reference to an all-powerful Creator who cared about their genitalia.

To discredit the claims of Protestantism completely, a group of intrepid Snesenologists conducted a landmark study on the number of souls in the afterlife who had died a sudden unex-pected death and compared their self-reported religious affil-iations during life. They hypothesized that if death came sud-denly—for instance, due to a violent crime, an explosion, or during sleep—there wasn't any time for a last minute conver-sion to Protestantism. Their seminal paper 'On the distribution of representatives of different faiths in the beyond compared to self-reported affiliation in life - Thirty case studies of sudden death' by Bennett and Brunel, published in Nature Snesenology, was the last nail in the coffin of Protestantism's exclusive claim to the afterlife [17]. Thus Protestantism was again reduced to one of the many faiths that laid claim to the beyond. Worldwide unrest subsided. The remaining faiths of the world were so relieved the Protestants had been proven wrong that no one dared raise the issue for some years. But the proverbial genie was out of the bottle. It was only a matter of time until another community of faith would try to claim this afterlife as their own, trying to sway more believers in its favour.

But what about the criminals? The subject was generally not talked about after the recent controversy. The presence of the wicked in what used to be thought of as heaven is the key for a meaningful interpretation of what was about to unfold. The general fear that some reincarnation-based faith would soon make its move brought the great monotheistic faiths of the world back together. Most historians of Snesenology believe that they reluctantly formed a new alliance, focusing on resolving the issue of the wicked with the power of theological analysis. The key idea to emerge from these efforts was the concept of a divine plan. When pressed on the issue of the wicked, the representatives of the world's faiths stated that it somehow had to be part of God's plan. God's design had to be extended into the eternal afterlife. In fact, the issue was soon reframed as indirect evidence for a divine plan. Theologians rejoiced. A God that could not only envision a plan for our finite sojourn on Earth but also for the eternity that followed, had to be at least twice as magnificent as a lazy God who only had to take care of a plan for our finite earthly existence. This spawned many sophisticated academic treatises, some of which can be found in the yearly Proceedings of the ISS. Indeed the concept of a divine plan held much more importance than it seemed at that moment in time.

13

Critics

While most people, experts and layman alike, had partaken in the public discourse on faith physics, one particular part of society had remained notably silent. Possibly encouraged by the scandalous finding that criminals reside in the afterlife, critics of religion finally made themselves heard again.

Before Alfred Snesenon provided empirical proof for the existence of the afterlife, these smug, arrogant, and shrill people had attacked religion around the world. Especially after the decline of pre-Snesenon science these vocal critics had a difficult time, and the fragile beginnings of something like a global, secular civil society had withered away quickly. Most people had given up atheism in the face of undeniable evidence for the afterlife. 'Atheist' became a synonym for people in denial. The only people worse off were the remaining *true agnostics*. Nevertheless, the lack of easy explanations for some of the mysteries of faith physics was striking. Many talented scholars had failed to offer convincing hypotheses. Alfred Snesenon's absence was being felt.

The overwhelming evidence in favour of the afterlife notwithstanding, some die-hard critics of religion continued to campaign for a so-called rational worldview. Encouraged by the lack of leadership in the faith physics community they organized panel discussions in town halls and universities. The turnout was usually meagre at best. Things took a turn for the better when Christopher Hitchens' Snesenon signature was discovered. In a twist of genius, the elderly Richard Dawkins invited the recently deceased Christopher Hitchens to give lectures from the afterlife with the help of a portable Snesenon engine. Hitch, as his dwindling supporters called him, acquired new fame and impressed even his critics. He is widely credited as the first person ever to author a book from the beyond. 'Even if he runs the show, he is still not great' became an instant bestseller but was mistaken by some for satire [18]. Nevertheless, Hitchens was once again respected, this time even by his enemies. It took real guts to lecture about the idiocy of superstition and the belief in the supernatural from the afterlife. Hitchens, never afraid to confront a tough audience, simply reversed his prior arguments. Given the fact that the dead were watching over the living, Hitch - still criticizing the notion of an all—seeing God as a celestial North Korea—now simply stated 'I told you so.' This provoked criticism and even copyright infringement claims from the Holy See.

The dwindling number of critics of religion was closely aligned with another part of society. Ever since the society had become aware of the heavenly overseers, some people wished not to pass into the afterlife after their deaths. It took only a few years for this sentiment to develop into a full-blown rebellion against heaven. Some people wanted to die in peace and be done with it forever. Led by the old critics the Let-Us-Die-In-Peace movement (usually abbreviated as LUDIP movement) formed. For a brief period the LUDIPs argued for

a destruction of all Snesenon engines. But this defeatist atti-
tude was discarded quickly. The dead would continue to watch
us. The LUDIPs acquired an unexpectedly big following. Their
demands resonated with every person that was terrorized by
the all-seeing eyes in the sky. More and more followers took
the leap and stopped seeing the prospect of eternal life as a
blessing. They marched in the streets yelling slogans like the
ever popular 'Just let us die and be done with it!', 'My life is
mine and nobody else's!', or simply 'I've had enough of my
fellow humans during life!' The media were torn between sym-
pathy and disdain.

Ever since the unfortunate case of Felipe Gonzales, thera-
pists the world over had been busy like never before. Now they
also had to deal with people who dreaded seeing old school
friends, work colleagues, and certain family members in the
afterlife and not ever being able to escape their annoying
habits—for eternity. Psychologists coined the term 'mother-
in-law syndrome' for this condition [19]. It did not take long
for the intellectual wing of the movement to develop ideas
about how the theory underlying the construction of Snesenon engines might be used to alter, perhaps even destroy,
the dimension that housed the afterlife. However, the ener-
gies to even attempt something like this lay far beyond the
capabilities of the human race. Nevertheless, the movement
was doing well. But a brutal act of violence led to its disin-
tegration. A mental patient who had recently been released
from the local psychiatry unit attacked its leader, the ageing
Richard Dawkins. It is an irony of fate that Dawkins was struck
with a tome of his collected hate mail. It remains a mystery
how the assailant was able to swing the 15,000-page book at
Dawkins' head without anybody intervening. Dawkins recovered but became a recluse after this brutal act. He continued

to publish books and pamphlets criticizing religion, but to his own dismay they were marketed as postmodernist critiques of the currently dominant world-view, unwittingly making him an edgy underground star in humanities departments around the world.

We have briefly touched upon the issue of mental patients further above. Why were so many mentally impaired people roaming the streets? This was a consequence of the ground-breaking psychological study of Hybsi and Norber [20]. By comparing the reports of schizophrenics with recorded inter-views that had been conducted by Snesenon engineering crews, the two researchers were able to establish that 95 per cent of schizophrenics with severe (so-called) hallucinations had genuine contact with the afterlife every time they heard voices. Apparently their brains had developed a natural sen-sitivity to the Snesenon effect and were able to perceive the souls in the beyond. They had simply been misdiagnosed. Thus after millennia hearing voices in your head was not an exclu-sive prerogative of clergy and prophets any more. Nevertheless, many of these people were deeply troubled as a result of years of meaningless therapy and unnecessary pharmacological treatments. At the height of the LUDIP movement, the streets had been full of people with such mental disorders (we should rather call them special abilities). Some had even reached posi-tions of political leadership.

The LUDIP movement never quite recovered from the loss of its charismatic leader. But the seeds of discontent were sown. Many people did not look forward to eternity in the beyond any more. With privacy gone and the prospect of an undesir-able eternity many people were inclined to choose suicide. Of course that would be highly counterproductive since it would only hasten the arrival in the afterlife. This discouraged the overwhelming majority of people from taking their own lives. For some religions it was the ultimate triumph. The emerging divine world order was self-enforcing. It enforced its own prohibition of suicide by virtue of its existence.

14

The Injection Point

After the LUDIP movement dissipated many of its members resigned themselves to a fatalist existence, accepting the inevitability of eternal life. Key figures of the movement now turned to scientific questions, which had previously seemed settled. Many formerly accepted theories had to be re-examined in the light of the recent discoveries. The list is long, and we have to restrict ourselves to the most interesting cases.

The most obvious choice for a theory that needed to be revisited was the theory of evolution by natural selection. In accordance with the false induction paradox all the bio-molecular, genetic, and paleontological evidence still pointed to evolution being true. Most followers of the world's major faiths, armed with the notion of Crime-Scene-Cleaning-Creator-Miracles and content with the empirical confirmation of the beyond, freely admitted that all evidence pointed to evolution being true and then went on with their lives.

Since evolution was still considered scientific fact[15], it raised an extremely interesting question that had never come up before.

15   See Chapter 17 for the updated stance taken by creationists.

At what moment in time during the course of human evolution had souls started departing into the afterlife? Or in other words: at what moment during evolution had God injected spirit into humans? Had he done it at the transition from one specific genus of homo to the next? Or when we developed language? Or had it all started with mammals? Had spirit been injected into bacteria? Soul-carrying bacteria? Or even soul-carrying self-replicating molecules? It was a mystery, but at least it kept the disillusioned LUDIPs occupied.

An interesting corollary of these brand new ideas was that Homo Habilis, Homo Erectus or even Australopithecus might be found in the beyond. Had they entered the afterlife? Did they carry souls? What about Neanderthals? And how could we test this question if a given subspecies had no language? At the time these were purely academic questions because no Snesenon engine could resolve the signatures of souls that had departed into the beyond so long ago. But was it theoretically possible to use some future advanced Snesenon engine to home in on the Snesenon signature of a specimen of Homo Erectus? Would he or she utter some grunt? Or did they not possess immortal souls? When then had souls started to appear in our world and subsequently depart into the beyond? To cut a long story short, the matter remains unresolved, but many high profile theological institutions keep funding research programs to tackle this question.

However, this new wave of scientific investigations into the afterlife clashed not only with the orthodoxies of the various denominations of Christianity, with Judaism and Islam. No, vocal and even violent opposition came from Buddhists, who finally began to argue that the contact with souls in the beyond was proof of reincarnation. The great Lama himself published several authoritative essays on the subject [21, 22]. The main argument in support of this notion was that hitherto it had been impossible to find a soul in the afterlife that had belonged to a long deceased person. This was taken as proof that souls do not stay long in the beyond but must return to Earth to be reincarnated in new vessels. In a particularly charged atmosphere, the Buddhist delegation vowed never to participate again in an ISS conference. The Great Lama ordered his brightest students to defend reincarnation with strong intellectual arguments. To avoid having to admit that the population growth of the past millennia required the continuous creation of new souls, the Buddhists had to postulate that the total number of souls was constant and that a rise in number of human souls across the millennia was proof of continuing self-improvement. Karma was improving on average. Given the constant heavenly surveillance this was hard to swallow for many. In addition, by extension this meant that the further one went into the past, the more souls must have been in vessels of lower form. Lower vertebrates, invertebrates, even bacteria. This provoked strong opposition from other organized religions, resulting in big rallies, with slogans like 'I am not a monkey soul!' or 'My mother was not a bacterium!' being chanted. In addition, there was a plain mathematical problem [23]. It seemed that the total number of living things had been smaller in the early history of the Earth and that the number of living creatures had continuously grown. This problem could only be solved by postulating that all souls had inhabited inanimate objects before transitioning to self-replicating molecules and eventually to bacteria. We can imagine that very bad karma might lead to reincarnation as a rock. However, it is difficult to conceive how a rock could act to improve his Karma in order to transition to the higher, nobler bacterial form. In a similar vein, it is also interesting to ponder how a bacterium improves its karma.

Nevertheless, the proponents of reincarnation were the only ones who were able to offer a coherent account of everything that was known about the souls in the beyond. Reincarnation fit the facts. It explained why criminals were in the afterlife and why members of all faiths were in the afterlife. They were all awaiting reincarnation. The day dreaded by the leaders of all other faiths, except Hinduism, had finally come. But further confirmation of reincarnation theory was hard to come by. Once a soul had moved on to a new vessel it was gone from the afterlife. Continued conversations with souls simply provided an upper bound for estimates on how long the souls lingered before moving on. Since contact with any given soul was lost sooner or later, this method of measuring the permanence of souls in the beyond was limited.

However, all this changed when a team of Snesenologists at Los Alamos, testing a new experimental Snesenon engine, found Bertrand Russell in the beyond. He was the oldest departed soul yet to be discovered in the afterlife. This cast a first shadow of doubt on Reincarnation Theory. At first it was hard to get any information out of him. Russell kept complaining about not being credited enough, together with other important critics of religion, by the so-called new atheists. But eventually he could be interviewed. He was quizzed about his attitudes towards religion, which he had so often expressed eloquently in his writings. With anguish he conceded that he had been wrong. Though he said he could not comment on the details, he is quoted as having said 'I was wrong! God's plan does indeed involve Hitler, the holocaust and the A-bomb!'

The discovery of Russell's soul was doubly important. First, he was the first departed soul to ever mention God's plan, a concept we will explore in more detail in the following chapter. Secondly, his mere existence in the afterlife set a new upper bound for how long a soul could linger in the afterlife if one assumed that all souls must eventually be reincarnated. It was briefly contemplated that Russell might have reached Nirvana. But the case for reincarnation weakened further when a new generation of Snesenon engines was able to contact Marc Twain, Pope John Paul II, Mahatma Gandhi, Avicenna, and eventually Attila the Hun. The existence of these long departed souls in the afterlife was the deathblow to reincarnation theory. Similarly to Catholics and Protestants, Buddhists were unable to sustain their claim on the afterlife. But more importantly, Russell's revelations about a divine plan held a profound message.

15

Leibniz

The deeper meaning behind Bertrand Russell's comments about God's plan did not go unnoticed. He seemed to imply that he had some form of knowledge about the Creator's design. It was here that most scholars suspected the solutions to all the outstanding mysteries of Snesenology. But when pressed for this knowledge Russell began talking about teapots. He either would not or could not reveal more information. Nevertheless, this moment has to be seen as a key turning point in the history of faith physics. The events surrounding the LUDIP movement and the reincarnation debate could not hide that Snesenology had stagnated for many years. The loss of Alfred Snesenon had been a severe blow to the field. His disciples had not yet stepped forward. Now Russell had implicitly revealed that there was indeed a divine plan. It remained concealed from us, but this was nevertheless a monumental discovery. In fact, his revelation is widely agreed to mark the end of the short period of classical faith physics. The eventual incorporation of the incredibly powerful notion of a divine plan into the theoretical edifice of Snesenology belongs to the era of modern faith physics, which is still on-going.

The publication of Russell's interviews rekindled the enthusiasm of early ISS conferences. Maybe there was even a way to uncover God's plan. After an extraordinary Snesenology meeting in Stockholm, the ISS announced a new concerted research effort. Buddhists were welcomed back to the meetings, and Snesenologists around the world were called upon to use their engines to find the one man who could possibly shed even more light on the Creator's plan. That man was Gottfried Wilhelm Leibniz.

As it is often the case in science, Leibniz had initially acquired fame for the wrong reasons. One of these was that he co-invented infinitesimal calculus, in parallel with Sir Isaac Newton [24,25]. But now he was sought because of his writings on the Theodicy [26]. Faced with the problem of suffering and evil in a world created by an almighty, all-knowing and loving God, Leibniz developed the notion of Theodicy. It consists of the idea that the universe in its current state is, in a restricted sense, the best possible world that God could have created. With regard to the good of the inhabitants of that universe, all suffering, all its imperfections—like war, starving children, HIV, poverty, child rape, and natural disasters—are determined by the necessary interactions of the constituent parts and cannot be avoided. God's creation is constrained by the necessary interactions he envisioned, except, of course, when he performs miracles. However, there were other contenders for the solution of the problem of evil. Leibniz's Theodicy had two main competitors. First, an intricate version of Demon Theory (DT) [27]. Some theologians postulated that the devil's forces were engaged in a continuous effort to thwart the Creator's design. Despite an all-powerful God, the agents of Beelzebub would thus corrupt and influence ordinary people to do bad things and tempt them into disbelief. This theory had some appeal because it elegantly explained the lack of humanitarian support in poverty-stricken and disease-ridden parts of the world. Money and development aid could not defeat the devil. Prayer was much more efficient. The second contender was Free Will Theory (curiously not abbreviated FWT but rather WTF) [28]. In this sophisticated theory it was the free will of human beings that led to suffering despite God's well-meaning plan. In a way, WTF was the most parsimonious of all theories because it placed less burden on both the Creator and humanity. But there seemed to be little space for a divine plan in WTF. Sure, the gaps could be plugged by crime-scene-cleaning-miracles, but ultimately this theory fell out of favour quickly once Leibniz's soul had been contacted, not least because most people preferred not to have free will attributed to them. For a while a hybrid theory WTF-DT was proposed [29], since free will and being corrupted by the devil's forces needed to go hand in hand. Divine retribution theory (where God punishes, e.g. via natural disasters or diseases like Malaria) cannot really be classified as a third contender because it was compatible with both WTF and DT. But none of these theories, despite their appeal to reason and logic, could account for a divine plan as elegantly as Theodicy.

Enter Leibniz. With the reach of modern government-funded Snesenon engines, it had finally become conceivable that contact to the soul of someone as long deceased as Leibniz might persist for a reasonable amount of time. After several years of soul-searching, Leibniz had indeed been found. Members of the ISS were overjoyed. Their efforts had paid off. Everybody wanted to ask about the high castle of Leibniz. In an unprecedented media event a press conference was organized with Leibniz himself speaking through a new Snesenon engine. Leibniz did not just give a hint like Russell. The reader may be aware that Leibniz is widely known to be the first departed soul ever to have directly revealed something about the nature of the afterlife. Sadly, like other souls, he too would not delve into any details, but he was happy to confirm his Theodicy. Suddenly there was no more need to combat poverty, prevent wars, or try to cure deadly diseases. We are indeed living in the best of all possible worlds. This was hailed by many as the first truly positive message from the after-life. Theodicy released many humans from a great burden. If it was correct then we could finally stop trying to improve our circumstances in life, to educate and better ourselves. Given God's perfection, Theodicy was the only sensible explanation for the existence of suffering in the world. Leibniz is quoted as saying that he finally felt vindicated now that the living had discovered the afterlife and that he was able to confirm his earlier theories for us. Theologians everywhere, even across faiths, were ecstatic. Leibniz's Theodicy now seemed like a much bigger deal than that puny infinitesimal calculus of his. Indeed, in a last interview before we lost contact with him he expressed some regrets about his life of scholarship. He is quoted as saying 'Imagine, had I devoted less of my precious time on Earth to meaningless nonsense like calculus, how many wonderful ideas equivalent to Theodicy I could have come up with.' However, when asked about the Creator Leibniz struggled for words and finally fell silent. No details about the Almighty could be extracted from him. This added to the mystery of the silent God. Still, Leibniz's revelations constitute a substantial conceptual advance in the fields of faith physics and theology.

16

Before Christ

In our historic account of Snesenology we have now reached the last few years prior to the writing of the present text. We can now take stock of what we have learned so far. Professor Snesenon's seminal work has been confirmed beyond any reasonable doubt by a multitude of contacts with the beyond, three of which we have looked at in more detail. Those were the stories of Anita Fromm, James Boyle, and Faruk Warsi. We have seen how these discoveries have driven the rise in number of the empiricist faithful and how they revolutionized science and theology, ultimately culminating in the founding of the International Society for Snesenology. We have thoroughly reviewed several examples of the continued competition among the world's faiths to lay claim to the hereafter. But it should also have become clear that Snesenology has always been strongly driven by technological advancements. Improving Snesenon engines helped reveal that the dead are watching over us, which became one of the key reasons for Alfred Snesenon's suicide. Snesenon's intellectual heirs had not yet stepped forward, and theoretical faith physics stagnated for a while. But as Snesenon engines continued to improve, they helped refute the monopolizing claims of Protestants and

Buddhists. Most importantly, advanced Snesenon engines put us in contact with Bertrand Russell and Gottfried Wilhelm Leibniz, allowing us to get a first glimpse at the grand designs of the Creator. These discoveries inaugurated the era of modern faith physics. Nevertheless, the uninitiated reader may have built up the impression that most discoveries of faith physics discussed so far did not really contribute to our well-being. This could not be further from the truth. The confirmation of Leibniz's Theodicy is a reminder of what we have gained through faith physics. Just imagine the perverse morals of people advocating for a worldview where earthquakes struck unsuspecting humans due to continental drift, rather than the best possible world design of the Creator.

It should not come as a surprise that Leibniz's Theodicy was gratefully accepted by most believers. For a time different Christian denominations tried to derive some legitimation from this fact. After all, Leibniz had been a Christian and had even endeavoured to reconcile the Roman Catholic and Lutheran churches before he died. Muslims and Jews objected immediately. Leibniz's explanation for suffering in the world, they contended, could be applied equally well to their religions. Many were even offended that someone would rather attribute earthquakes, tsunamis, and genetic defects that strike unsuspecting families, to the best possible world-design of a Christian God instead of Allah or Yahweh. They argued that both were equally capable in designing this best of all universes. This even threatened to disturb the fragile peace among faiths and their renewed research efforts agreed upon at the recent Stockholm conference.

The scope of this limited introduction to the history of faith physics does not allow me to mention all the great historical figures which have been subsequently discovered in the afterlife. Each new generation of Snesenon Equipment allowed the operators to reach deeper into the past. But the above-mentioned problem was exacerbated when, inspired by the contact with Leibniz, Christians finally set out to contact the soul of Jesus himself. The hope was that Jesus would shed some light on the nature of God's plan. The architects of this audacious endeavour relied on the notion that Jesus was part of the Holy Trinity. Since we nowadays have proof of the afterlife, the reader is forgiven for not remembering the details of the doctrine of the Holy Trinity from their religious education classes. I will recapitulate briefly.

The Trinity defines God as three consubstantial persons or expressions: the Father, the Son, and the Holy Spirit. It is one God in three persons. But the reader should not be confused. The three are distinct, yet are one substance. As the Fourth Lateran Council stated, 'it is the Father who generates, the Son who is begotten, and the Holy Spirit who proceeds'. When they are not distinct, they are one, co-equal, co-eternal and con-substantial. And, of course, each is God, whole and one. There. It is that simple. The godly is the nature, or 'what' one is. The individual aspects are the persons, or 'who' one is. If the reader cannot see the simple logic behind this elegant reshuffling of interrogative pronouns, I can offer the following analogy. The Holy Trinity is the central mystery of Christianity. Now let us imagine one is tasked with solving a difficult mathematical problem. If the result doesn't make sense to the thinking mind, we are clearly justified in concluding that one has stumbled across a central mystery of mathematics.

Unfortunately, Jesus' soul has not yet been found. Some the-ologians speculate that this may be because, being part of the Trinity, finding Jesus would be akin to finding God himself, which has proven very difficult. But this view contained an implicit rec-ognition of the doctrine of the Trinity. Thus this critique was not available to non-Christian faiths.

While the search for Jesus was on-going, Snesenologists from South Africa had realized a startling fact. There is a strong correlation between the time since departure into the afterlife of a soul and the coherence of its Snesenon signature. The older a deceased soul is, the more difficult it is to establish contact. The Snesenon signatures become fuzzier, more difficult to isolate. However, this also meant that the fuzziness could be used as an age estimate. The race to find ever-older departed souls was on, despite the inability to locate the soul of Jesus. It was hoped that by delving deeper and deeper into the past, one might at least encounter some of the protagonists from the many stories in the various holy books. Representatives of the three main Abrahamic religions all tried to find support for their respective unique words of God. For the Old Testament, the oldest recorded sources are still the Dead Sea Scrolls, dated between 408 BC and 318 BC. So when Snesenologists in the Vatican started targeting Snesenon signatures that appeared to date roughly from that period, they had high hopes. The probability of success had been small to begin with, but when they finally isolated a Snesenon signature (a difficult feat in itself) the disappointment was tremendous. The Snesenon signature turned out to belong to the ancient Greek philosopher Plato, whose life ended in the same timeframe, sometime in the 4th century BC. Plato was alive when the stories of the Old Testament were still told and written down in the Middle East.

The Snesenologists of the Vatican had hoped for so much. They could have encountered the protagonists of some of the wonderful stories from the Old Testament. Stories like the insightful instructions for curing skin conditions like leprosy, found in the book of Leviticus. Just find two small birds, kill one and drain its blood and organs into a bowl. Then use the other bird to stir the blood and organ cocktail and apply the soaked bird to the portion of your skin that is affected [30]. Simple. Transparent. Beautiful. Instead they were faced with the meaningless drivel of some bearded Greek who wrote hundreds of pages about logic, truth, justice, love and beauty, and similar intellectual shamanism. It may be a bit unfair to simply cherry-pick the text passages where Plato pursues nonsensical inquiries into the nature of morality, the difference between knowledge and belief, or the value of free inquiry, and so forth, but it does serve to underline the startling difference in clarity of mind and outlook on the world between a confused Plato and the clear and transparent writings of the Old Testament. It was a stark reminder of what faith physics had done for the world by linking the sphere of theology to empirical inquiry. It also anticipates the positive message and ultimate salvation provided by the discoveries of quantum soul theory, which I will outline for the reader in the final chapter.

After listening to Plato for some time, who would possibly want to emphasize the contribution of Greek, Roman, and so-called enlightenment thinking to European civilization? No! The principle defining characteristic of Europe is its Judeo-Christian heritage. But Plato just wouldn't shut up and instead told naughty stories of his gay exploits. Plato is famously known to be the first soul in the afterlife on which Snesenon engine operators hung up in frustration. Who could blame them?

17

Holy Gaps

While the search for Jesus is still on-going, Leibniz's revelations of a supreme divine plan led other people to raise anew the question of design. At this point, no sane person doubted any longer that some supreme being had created the universe. But there were different proposals as to how and when this creation had occurred.

The most vocal proponents of design proposed young Earth creation[16] and intelligent design. If the world had a divine plan, why not assume young Earth creation in the first place? Or in other words: what evidence was there really to exclude the possibility that the Earth was just 6000 years old? In the end this was a concealed effort to swing the public opinion in favour of one particular faith, just like the Vatican's secret project and the failed attempts by Protestants and Buddhists.

According to the creationist account time began in 4004 BC with the creation of the world and Adam. Young Earth creationists borrowed a well-established tactic from the moderates. If miracles could be accounted for by the Crime-Scene-Cleaning-

---

16 The notion that the farthest star or galaxy is about 6000 light-years away.

Creator, then a similar godly device could account, for instance, for the presence of fossils. The Creator could have created the young Earth with fossils already in place. Others argued that fossils had been deposited during the great flood, implying that dinosaurs had co-existed with pre-flood humanity. In either case, the crime scene was clean from the outset. Incidentally, this led to declarations of respect from Muslim creationists and even provoked some Christian purists to join the young Earth creationists because they were the only ones to uphold the true glory and virtue of earthly religion: belief not only in the absence of evidence but in spite of evidence to the contrary.

The glorious struggle against the tyranny of logic seemed to succeed. Some people looked up to the creationists because of this staunch defence of common sense. But the truth is that despite these highly appealing arguments an overwhelming majority of people just did not care about the age of the Earth and the issue of evolution, now that the afterlife was a reality. It all seemed to have little impact on their daily routine, which now usually started with personal hygiene in complete darkness. The confirmed existence of the afterlife had fostered total indifference to evolution. 'So what?' most ordinary people asked themselves. It was not important anymore how we got here, be it guided theistic evolution, intelligent design and young Earth creation or plain old Darwinian evolution, foreseen by the Almighty in all its interactions. Furthermore, it seemed like there was no easy way to decide on the issue. The creationist claim to represent the one true religion would have been one among many such claims had it not been for one intriguing fact. Only young Earth creation seemed to resolve the problem of the injection point, which we have encountered above.

The international faith physics community was suddenly faced with two well supported—if competing—claims. The first was that Christian young Earth creationism was indeed correct. The obvious objection that not only Christians had been found in the afterlife was raised. But Christian creationists attributed these to deliberate deceptions by the forces of the devil, posing as non-Christians. The second claim was that Muslim young Earth creationism was indeed correct. Again the objection was raised that not only Muslims had been found in the afterlife. But Muslim creationists attributed these to deliberate deceptions by the forces of the devil, posing as non-Muslims. These claims were hard to counter, but once again Snesenology saved the day. Shortly after the discovery of Leibniz and Plato, an accident with a Snesenon engine in Cape Town helped to settle the issue of intelligent design and young Earth creation once and for all. A freak event with a new experimental Snesenon engine was responsible. Due to the unfortunate coincidence of human error and faulty cabling the machine built up its energy levels to an unprecedented height, causing a meltdown in a nuclear power plant in the process. But before the breakdown of the equipment, the local engineering team was able to focus their instruments on an extremely old Snesenon signature and establish contact. The soul spoke in a strange language. The issue hardly seemed worth mentioning. It had happened before that the signatures of souls, which spoke in strange languages, had been picked up. Sooner or later the language was always identified as some obscure and almost extinct language. But this time no one was able to identify the language. Eventually the recording was published with the hope that some clever individual would decipher it one day. Two years passed until late last year Dr. Andros Prunitos, hitherto known as an expert on the digestive tract of New Zealand seals, deciphered the meaning [31]. He decomposed the language into phonemes and meticulously tried matching combinations of them to any known written script. After years of study, including

121

comparisons to previous transliterations of the various cunei-form Sumerian scripts, he published his findings. The language had to be Sumerian.

The freak event at Cape Town had established a link to the oldest deceased soul yet. A bold research team replicated the conditions of the Cape Town Event, this time with better power supply. Prunitos then interviewed the Sumerian. It was difficult to converse with such an ancient man, but eventually his time of death could be inferred from his knowledge on astronomy. He also pointed archaeologists to hitherto undiscovered Sumerian ruins, which were dated to the corresponding time. The upshot of the whole enterprise was that Sumerians really had existed more than 6000 years ago. But more importantly, the operating condi-tions of this modified Snesenon engine allowed Snesenologists to correlate more precisely than ever before the various parameters of a working Snesenon engine with the age (since death) of a targeted Snesenon signature. The correlation was confirmed on all hitherto contacted Snesenon signatures, including individ-uals the creationists themselves considered genuine. Thus the same machines that had confirmed the existence of the afterlife beyond any doubt had contacted the soul of a man who had lived before 4004 BC. A previously unthinkable feat, Snesenology had effectively discredited young Earth creationism. Some die-hard supporters claimed that this was the final test of the Creator, that it was indeed the devil talking, tempting us into disbelieve, that the very foundations of the mathematical analyses were not to be trusted. One had to believe in spite of the talking Sumerian, despite mathematics, despite empirical contradictions. But this was a minority position. Creationists had publicly committed to faith physics and its revelations about the afterlife long ago. This included its empirical foundations. There was no way to recon-cile the age estimate with their views. However, in a stroke of genius the most famous proponents of intelligent design saved the movement and the financial structure of its institutions by inventing a new narrative. According to the new doctrine creationist teachings had always been intended as satire [32]. Still today Christian and Muslim creationists rank among the best and most respected satirists and comedians in the world.

18

Original Innocence

Our historical account of faith physics is quickly approaching the present day, and the greatest revelations (not yet widely known outside of academia) are yet in store for us. Despite the various failed attempts of different religious communities to claim the Snesenon realm as their own afterlife, the notion of a divine plan has by now taken root in the collective consciousness. But the fact that all faiths which tried had failed to monopolize the afterlife led Snesenologists to finally refocus their efforts on the problem of mutual exclusivity of religions. This exclusivity is but one aspect of what is called the common sense paradox.

Ever since the first conversations with departed souls scholars have been plagued by a lingering doubt. How could it be that the afterlife contained Christians like Pope John Paul II, Hindus like Mahatma Gandhi, as well as members of other faiths? Wasn't Gandhi supposed to be in hell (at least according to some religions)? The same type of argument was put forth by Muslims concerning Faruk Warsi, Avicenna, and others. If Avicenna was in the afterlife, how could Christians and Hindus be there too? Finding these old souls among the departed thus had repercussions far beyond the reincarnation issue. It is also true that the recent research into the problem of mutually exclusive religions is in part due to the fact that this matter has always bothered some of the empiricist faithful. One can say a lot about these previously moderate believers, but few of them would argue that a man like Gandhi deserved to go to hell just because he happened to have followed a competing faith before his death. But if followers from all religions were to be found in the afterlife, how could it be decided which religion was the correct one? Were they not mutually exclusive? Official representatives of most faiths reluctantly took this stance when pressed on the issue, while many believers ignored this state of affairs and focused on the more heart-warming aspects of their religion. This is the problem that we know today as the common sense paradox [33]. Some people even went as far as to call it the common moral sense paradox, since it was clearly morally reprehensible that any innocent and compassionate man or woman (let alone an innocent child) would be condemned to eternal torment just because they had been brought up in the wrong religion, as determined by the accident of their birth. This is also why some people called the CSMP the innocence-at-birth-problem. Catholic scholars were tempted to point out that original sin provided a perfect explanation, calling the innocence-at-birth-problem a perverse inversion of logic. But this point of view was never emphasized publicly, because it clashed with evolving morality. No, most scholars reasoned that there had to be a simple solution to this problem. The reader may be disappointed to read this, but to this day no one knows how to resolve the common moral sense paradox. In fact, at the moment the common moral sense paradox is largely an academic issue, which is why you may not have heard about it at all. Nonetheless, the attentive reader may have caught on to the matter much earlier. After all even Christopher Hitchens was in this afterlife. How was it possible that an atheist and heretic like him had made it into the beyond? It is puzzling to find these departed souls in the afterlife of the one true silent God (even if we don't know which one). But most people simply do not have the time to consider such issues. They worry about being harassed by their deceased loved ones and do not care much for these theological subtleties. Given the troubles of life, it is too much to wonder why the followers of any particular religion were or were not among the beatified dead, right beside departed Christians, Hindus, Muslims, Pastafarians, Rastafarians, Jews, Buddhists, followers of Zeus, Isis, Wotan, Thor, Mithras, The Great Talking Stone of Anatolia, The Fire-Breathing Purple Chicken of Cyprus and about 9985 other deities. And, to be fair, most ordinary people—if they happen to have heard about the common moral sense paradox at all—do not resent the fact that perfectly innocent people who happened to be born into a different religion are to be found in the afterlife. We will touch upon the common moral sense paradox again further below, when I discuss my own scholarly work as part of the introduction to the cutting edge of faith physics, for I believe to have found a possible solution to the paradox.

For a while, the common moral sense paradox had disappeared even from academic discourse, until more prominent opposition figures were discovered in the afterlife. As it turned out Christopher Hitchens was only the tip of the iceberg. Notable other encounters included Salman Rushdie and Ludwig Feuerbach. How could these vocal critics of religion be present in the afterlife? People of faith were, as with the case of Hitchens, at first dismayed, even shocked to find these heretic figures in heaven. However, after a while some clever theologians thought they had gleaned an opportunity to confirm a particular faith. A sort of inverse rule of mutual exclusivity. This ingenious idea posits the following. One could make the case that the existence of critics of other religions in the afterlife is to be taken as evidence that the one religion not criticized can be considered implicitly confirmed. It was a creative way to approach the issue, but it was quickly pointed out that critics of religion, even if they placed emphasis on one particular faith, are critical of all religions.

Today the International Society for Snesenology offers a million-dollar prize for a solution to the common moral sense paradox, but so far no one has stepped forward. In my opinion the idea of the inverse rule, though original, cannot resolve the questions raised by advanced Snesenology. However, a new promising theory is on the horizon, and it is to the discussion of this theory that I have given a contribution myself. It is the first which tries to make sense of everything we have learned about the afterlife so far. But before we move to these issues I want to mention some important recent developments in faith physics. It is becoming increasingly clear that no account of the history of Snesenology can be considered complete without the story of the grandest genius since Alfred Snesenon. His star pupil has finally come forth, and he may be the one man who may one day put us in contact with the Almighty.

19

Summa Technologiæ

No one has dared something as audacious as building an engine supposedly capable of contacting the Almighty himself since the Vatican's secret project in advanced Snesenology and the failed crowd-funded attempt to build a new type of Snesenon engine. As far as we know the Holy See never made any substantial progress in finding hell or contacting God directly before the project was abandoned and disclosed. But it now seems that there is one man who may bring us closer to this goal. You have almost certainly not heard about him, for at this moment he is not yet well known outside of academia. This man is Dr. Zolt Zycra. Zycra was Alfred Snesenon's star pupil. He is the man who continued Snesenon's work after his suicide. For a long time he has laboured in isolation with the remainder of Snesenon's research lab. Only recently has he come forth to present his revolutionary work.

Zycra has been an admirer of Snesenon from an early age. Thanks to his diligent parents he had been familiarized with all the intricacies of heaven and hell even before he could write, let alone perform the sophisticated mathematics of faith physics. But as soon as his home schooling in earthly (and heavenly) matters had begun, he displayed a fantastic gift for higher mathematics. As it is often the case with genius, Zycra's mind worked in ways which were incomprehensible to others. It is said that already as a young child his nightmares about hell were filled with mathematical symbolism. Later in life he used his own household Snesenon equipment to regularly converse with the soul of C.G. Jung, hoping to receive guidance concerning his rich dreamscapes, not unlike Wolfgang Pauli in the search for the fine structure constant.

His talent had drawn the attention of Professor Snesenon when Zycra published his first articles in theoretical faith physics [34]. The grand old man of Snesenology had invited the young Zycra to work under his guidance. Together Zycra and Snesenon were a formidable team. Before Snesenon died they had worked tirelessly to extend quantum soul theory. As it is often the case in science, Professor Snesenon—despite his brilliance—had been set in his ways. It took Zycra's fresh, young mind to advance quantum soul theory. Zycra's unconventional approach under the guidance of the older and wiser Snesenon culminated in the biggest achievement of faith physics yet. Although it is too early to tell what exactly will come out if it, I am told[17] that Zycra's work may finally unlock the direct route to the Creator himself. I have to confess that, though I do not doubt the brilliance of this great scientist, I am sceptical. But if there ever was a man who can put us into contact with the Almighty, it has to be Zycra.

Based on the works of Snesenon, Zolt Zycra has postulated the Regress Field (nowadays also known as Zycra Field), which is supposed to connect the two parallel universes, the here and now and the beyond [35]. Ripples in the Zycra Field

---

17   Sadly even I cannot follow what is said to be the most exquisite mathematics since general relativity and early faith physics.

manifest as pilot waves that guide the souls into the beyond and convey quantum soul information between the dimensions. I have mentioned in the beginning that classical Snesenology is a purely descriptive theory. This new research is still in its infancy, but it constitutes the first theoretical developments in faith physics that may give a functional account of the connection between the worlds. But Zycra was not content with purely theoretical work. He wanted to derive practical applications from his modifications of the Snesenon equations. From what I can tell the Zycra Field appears to be a precondition for the Snesenon effect. After Professor Snesenon had taken his own life Dr. Zycra worked tirelessly to produce a new type of Snesenon engine. His work eventually culminated in the design of the Aquinas engine [36].

Similarly to the ill-fated commercial project by the former Bell engineers (and the Vatican's secret project), the Aquinas engine is supposed to be able to scan the afterlife in broad sweeps at a yet unrivalled scale. But instead of simply listening for the Creator's voice the Aquinas engine is supposed to track down the location of the Creator itself. The Aquinas engine relies on the hypothesis that the Regress Field vanishes at the location of the Creator. Interestingly, other qualities like goodness, beauty, and many others are postulated to be maximal at the Creator's location in the beyond. Unfortunately, the theory is difficult to test. First, because the energy necessary to run the Aquinas engine is still prohibitively high, and second, due to slower than expected progress in the building of a goodness or beauty meter (Zycra has outlined the principles necessary to construct a goodness meter in an appendix of his doctoral thesis [37]). It is tragic that Alfred Snesenon has not lived to see the final fruits of his pupil's labour, but everybody assumes that he is watching *from above.*

Strictly speaking, this concludes the account of the history of faith physics as it is widely agreed upon in academic circles. The preceding chapters outline the current understanding of Snesenology and a summary of the most important developments of the past years. But while we all wait for the Aquinas engine to be built we can speculate further on the nature of the afterlife and of the Creator. If you, the reader, have made it this far, you should also be able to follow—and I hope enjoy—the following chapter, which outlines some new and more unorthodox theories concerning the afterlife. These theories are highly controversial and were presented by various scholars (including myself) at this year's meeting of the International Society for Snesenology. I believe they constitute a substantial conceptual advance and may guide us in the use of the Aquinas engine, once it comes online.

20

Terra Incognita

With the false induction paradox[18] and common sense paradox[19] unresolved, and the Aquinas engine not yet ready, advanced Snesenology is stagnating again. However, some radical Snesenologists believe that we should not surrender our intellect to the readings of machines. They believe that all the important pieces of the puzzle are already on the table and allow us to draw a new, radical conclusion. I will briefly outline this new hot topic in faith physics, followed by my own opinion on these matters.

It would be foolish to deny the existence of the afterlife. Thanks to the Snesenon effect, the evidence in favour of the afterlife (dare I say heaven?) is overwhelming. Undeniable some would say. But with the noteworthy exception of Leibniz's revelations, most significant questions remain unanswered. Why is the Creator silent? When did souls start to depart into the beyond on evolutionary timescales? Which of the many competing earthly religions has a core of metaphysical ground truth beneath all its beautiful allegory? How can we resolve the common moral sense paradox?

18   The reader is reminded that the false induction paradox refers to the puzzling effectiveness of pre-Snesenon Science.

19   Or the common (moral) sense paradox.

In other words: why do we find followers of all religious faiths and atheists in this afterlife? These are not new questions. What could be the solution to these problems? If the Aquinas engine works these questions may very well be answered one day. But radical pragmatists believe that the entire accumulated body of knowledge about this afterlife needs to be reinterpreted. They suggest that the above evidence can only be compatible with one type of religion—a currently unknown religion [38]. By extension all present and past religious faiths would cover only limited aspects of this one *mother religion* (also called M-religion or M-theory). Since there is no such thing as a Christian Muslim or a Jewish Hindu, since nobody can produce evidence in favour of one faith over the other, and because they are all mutually exclusive to the point of condemning infidels to eternal torment, there must be— these radicals reason—a faith that encompasses all dogmas that have been proven to be true. There can be no other solution, they claim. To reframe the proposition: most people follow the faith of their parents or the dominant faith of the country they were born in. How then can they all be in the afterlife? Given that we have certain proof of the afterlife, the logical conclusion must be that we are in contact with the afterlife as envisioned by a yet undiscovered religion. An exquisite set of dogmatic prescriptions not yet imagined by any person in the history of humanity needs to be uncovered. The pragmatist radicals conclude that we have to synthesize the tenets of this unknown faith and that it needs to be compatible with the biographies of all the souls so far discovered to reside in the afterlife. It is the ultimate terra incognita of theological truths, also known as terra incognita theory or the final frontier of faith. It is *the* grand social project on which to embark. This year's ISS conference was the first to discuss this theory. Although it will no doubt be met with mild scepticism by the adherents of any particular faith, this is an intriguing, no, an outright inspiring and grandiose idea. It could also be the long sought-after explanation of why the deceased reveal so little about the hereafter.

Personally I find this approach highly appealing. It seems to be the only theory that can explain the common moral sense paradox. However, terra incognita theory has its own share of problems. Most likely even this theory cannot explain why criminals and atheists are to be found in this afterlife. However, I believe I have conceived of a valid alternative hypothesis. With all due modesty, I would like to offer this alternative interpretation for consideration at this point. It is, in a way, a variation of the terra incognita theory. But the original terra incognita theory is not too radical. It is not radical enough. I do not propose that all departed souls—which may be all of dead humanity as far as we know—are in the heaven of a yet unknown religion. I propose something else entirely. The only theory compatible with all the data is that all departed souls contacted thus far are in the hell of a yet unknown religion. Yes, that is correct. I propose that the soul of every human being that has ever lived resides in hell (or the vestibule of hell) and that the Snesenon effect has in fact allowed us to establish contact with this realm, and not with heaven.

The obvious objection to this idea would be that Leibniz and Russell apparently revealed that the Creator has a plan. Intuitively people automatically assume that this means that they reside in the Creator's domain, i.e. in heaven. But this is far from obvious in my opinion. They might just as well have acquired this information in hell, e.g. from the devil himself[20].

I realize my theory will no doubt be considered unorthodox even among radicals. However, I am not a misanthropist. I simply have to go where logic takes me. This version of the terra incognita theory explains more findings compared to the heavenly version

---

20   Curiously the gender of the devil is not disputed.

of the theory. Let me exemplify this with a brief discussion of the common sense paradox. In the context of this paradox you may entertain the idea that the hell-bound innocents at birth would constitute cruelty beyond measure on part of a Creator. Why would the Creator fashion a world where several billion people are doomed to spend eternity in hell through no fault of their own? This notion is exponentiated if all of humanity is destined for hell, until we envision the correct M-religion. However, Theodicy elegantly solves this problem. Its explanatory power goes beyond the problem of evil. It also absolves the Creator. The world cannot be made a better place by any changes to his divine design. Leibniz revealed to us that we are living in the best possible world. It may very well be that it is part of the plan that all souls go to this hell, until we have proven ourselves worthy by discovering the set of rituals and commandments we need to follow. This may be regrettable, but most importantly only hell-based terra incognita theory explains the silence of God and the presence of criminals in the afterlife. The latter two findings are not compatible with the heavenly terra incognita theory.

In all fairness it has to be said that both interpretations are highly controversial at the moment. Nevertheless, I hope to have given the reader some food for thought. At the very least I hope it has become clear that we are not doomed to wait for the Aquinas engine to be constructed. There is room for well-founded academic speculation. It may have led us to a mildly depressing conclusion, but I will do my best to end on a positive note in the next and final chapter. However, before I conclude this chapter I also want to mention briefly the problem of moral values, which is often neglected in other introductory texts on faith physics. Possibly the greatest tragedy of Snesenology is that it has the potential to finally pacify the world forever but has failed to do so. Ever since the afterlife has become a reality there was also the hope that contact with the Creator would allow us to confirm a set of absolute moral values. Until now, religious leaders and believers the world over have been very measured, careful not to profess absolute values, lest it may lead to conflict with other faiths that follow other absolute moral values or even with non-believers. Now absolute moral knowledge seems finally within reach. Some say that this is yet another problem that will be solved by the Aquinas engine. But I want to leave you with the proposition that maybe—just as with terra incognita theory—based on what we already know we can derive a set of moral teachings that is logically consistent with all the known findings about the afterlife. This joyful enthusiasm is not to say that these radical interpretations will solve all remaining mysteries. The world has undergone a profound change and most ordinary people are still puzzled. So many questions remain unanswered. Why did no departed soul ever talk directly about the Creator or the devil? And why has no one ever found a follower of the Purple Chicken of Cyprus in the afterlife? There are plenty of mysteries that await resolution. We should also not forget that these mysteries are largely academic issues. I have placed a strong emphasis on the disruptive consequences of faith physics as a novel and revolutionary science, which changed how we view the world. But it has to be admitted that many people are genuinely happy about the prospect of eternal life, wherever it may be. Fear of death has largely disappeared. Death now symbolizes a far away, long-dreaded family holiday, where everyone is united with their loved ones, whether they want to or not. Given this prospect, some people still fear death. But the classical, existential fear of death that had tormented people for so long is gone, my theorizing about hell notwithstanding. People may be fearful and self-censoring. They may speculate when during evolution the immortal soul had been injected into the living matter on the surface of the Earth or what purpose the rest of the cosmos serves. They may even speculate what they could do in the eternal afterlife. But at long last people finally behave in accordance with their justified beliefs.

141

21

A Silver Lining

The hypotheses espoused in the preceding chapter may be slightly unsettling to some readers. If my theory is correct, then hell awaits us all until we are able to infer the tenets of the unknown Mother Religion. However, I hope the reader appreciates that it was my intention, and my duty as a scholar, to give a complete and unbiased (as far as this is possible) account of faith physics, including the current hot topics in the field. Nevertheless, the reader can rest assured that there is a silver lining to all this. Whatever your misgivings about this afterlife revealed by Alfred Snesenon—be it your loved ones watching over you, the silence of the Creator, or any other of the unresolved problems—I want to leave you on a hopeful note. In order to accomplish this let me draw your attention to the false induction paradox.

We have briefly touched upon the false induction paradox when we discussed the decline of traditional, pre-Snesenon science that followed the discovery of the afterlife. Despite desperate attempts to embrace new methods of gathering knowledge, the scientific community is but a shadow of its former self. This is one of the many consequences of Snesenon's work. Yet, before the discovery of incontrovertible proof for the beyond, many scientists had not believed in an afterlife. Not even Stephen Hawking was able to reconcile the past success of science in explaining the phenomena of the natural world and in improving life circumstances with the fact that it had led most of its practitioners to hold false beliefs. This notion is at the core of the false induction paradox, and it is here where we begin to find the consolations of faith physics. I want to leave the reader with the idea that this decline of science and faulty pre-Snesenon logic is, in fact, a glorious development for all humankind.

Imagine the great Alfred Snesenon had never discovered quantum soul theory. We wouldn't even be aware of the fact that we need to search for the M-Religion. I dare say the discoveries of Snesenon and Zycra were our saving grace, for you may not know how narrowly we have escaped disaster. The reader may not have been aware of it, because of the glacial pace of societal change, but faith, the world over, was in dire straits before Alfred Snesenon made his discovery. Sure, men of faith everywhere had tried to stem the tide of a secular Zeitgeist and the dangerous idolization of pre-Snesenon science. Not enjoying any leftover privileges from the pious past, it was a difficult if righteous fight the believers had fought in a globalizing world. But the bitter truth is that a so-called humanistic and scientific worldview was winning the battle for the hearts and minds of the young. With each generation, the number of people that fell into the trap of coherent thinking was growing. With each generation more and more people had begun to associate the benefits of science, enjoyed in everyday life, with its (as we now know) pseudo-logical implications concerning the nature of the universe. The sublime image of humanity's place in a vast and beautiful cosmos revealed by modern astronomy, with all its melancholy and all its grandeur, and the unity of all life inferred from evolutionary theory and genetics were infecting more and more human minds with their so-called spiritual magnificence. So powerful was the dark allure of this worldview that some people even started to be content with not knowing everything about the universe. Sometimes they simply said 'I don't know.' Yes, that was the crazy world that was starting to take shape before the advent of Snesenology. Today all this is hard to believe. Luckily we now know that our brief sojourn on Earth is but a preparation for an eternity in the afterlife and that all those worlds in the cosmos are just a playful waste of space on the part of the Almighty.

Even on more practical levels things were changing for the worse before the Snesenonian revolution. The reader would be justified to ask how these people had thought to organize their societies. Surely these misguided individuals did not believe that pre-Snesenon science told them anything about how to live their lives or about the distinction between good and evil, which we are expecting to extract from the Creator once the Aquinas engine goes online. As a matter of fact, mostly they did not. Again, we have to thank Alfred Snesenon and his disciples for reviving the categorical notions of absolute morality, of good and evil. But the sad truth is that a large part of humanity had been living—unknowingly—in a world where the moral Zeitgeist was not divinely sanctioned anymore. How else—some of them had reasoned—was it possible to live in large societies with freedom of religion, freedom from religion, and freedom of speech? Peaceful co-existence of many peoples and ideas had required the emergence of ethics, which transcended mutually exclusive moral codes developed millennia ago in isolation. These deluded men and women valued above all the freedom of thought and speech, for without it there could be no intercourse, no exchange, no debate, and no synthesis in a pluralist society. Universal humanist values and human rights they had called their blinding pseudo-morality. Perversely, some had gone even further and had started to include animals in their moral musings, demoting humans to just another species. Most outrageously, it was often stated that if some of their values were shared with religious moral codes, they were to be found over and over again in the teachings of many thinkers throughout the history of humanity. The idea had arisen that there must be some innate, common, moral sense in humans, a force that counterbalances the natural impulses of fear and aggression in social mammals. This common empathy and sense of justice, paired with intelligence—it was said—provided the fertile ground for morals and ethics, which were not derived from divine authority and common to all human beings.

Today we enjoy the benefits of the revelations of Snesenon and Zycra, but before their discoveries it was a different world. The apparent explanatory power of science had led more and more people astray. The crux of the matter was that this misplaced trust in a logically consistent and intelligible universe, a universe in which causes could be understood and were not attributed to divine or demonic forces, was inextricably linked with the freedom of the individual. Some went as far as to call it a precondition, for freedom and fate were incompatible. Worse, free inquiry sooner or later breeds distrust in authority. Humanity had been led onto a slippery slope. Universal education, the humanism of the so-called Enlightenment, and the apparently self-correcting nature of the scientific method, had all conspired to misguide more and more people. Radicals even went as far as to renounce national and wider cultural boundaries. They argued that ideas like experimental science, philosophy, democracy, the rule of law, and citizenship were simply good ideas, human achievements, irrespective of their source. Enlightenment science, Greek philosophy, Arab astronomy, Indian mathematics ... they all could not be appropriated by single nations but were part of a wider human heritage. Anybody who studied and understood, anybody who appreciated these and many similar notions, could share in them, be part of them irrespective of the culture of origin of both the idea and the mind that contemplated it. Only through the accidental forces of history and geography had these achievements been confined to different isolated, walled-off patches of the Earth in different periods of history. It seemed as if good ideas spread, knew no boundaries, seemed not to care what people ate, how they dressed or what their songs were. Global information networks accelerated the spread of these ideas. Suddenly people did not need an ivory tower education anymore to be led astray. And the organized faiths of the world were helpless. The moral Zeitgeist had accepted education as a universal good. Nothing could be done against it. Only some global calamity could have reversed the trend. Alas, that was too much to hope for. The intellectual, moral and material constituents of this worldview were self-perpetuating. Start down this path of 'reason' once and you will suddenly find yourself explaining more and more previously mysterious phenomena. Enjoy the freedom of speech and ideas once and you will not be able to do without it any more. Travel the world once and you forever recognize the humanity of all peoples. Enjoy the Internet, antibiotics, and x-rays once and you will not want to do without them any longer. That is how it must have seemed to these people. Of course nowadays it is easy to call them foolish, but we must recall that they had been unaware of the false induction paradox.

We were indeed on a slippery slope. There was no middle ground. The scale cannot be held in balance. Once it had been tipped in favour of so-called reason, an unstoppable movement started gaining traction. That was the danger we were all in. But Alfred Louis Snesenon has shown us that a different world is possible. It is in this context that the reader has to evaluate and appreciate all of faith physics and everything you have read on the preceding pages. Snesenon and Zycra stopped the avalanche, the onslaught of misguided reason. We have to be eternally grateful to these two scholars. We are truly standing on the shoulders of giants. By giving us irrefutable evidence for the afterlife they have destroyed the credibility of pre-Snesenon science and everything it supported. They saved us from certain disaster and from gradually abandoning our justified belief in the afterlife and its Creator. They have restored the trust in the authority of men who can interpret divine wisdom and cleanse us from sin. But most importantly they delivered us from the burden of freedom. Your hard-won, truly enlightened acceptance of the beyond, with all its subtle consequences, dear reader, should never be taken for granted. Never forget that it is principally owed to the work of the two great thinkers, Snesenon and Zycra.

REFERENCES

[1] A. L. Snesenon - The Quantum Soul Postulate: an Information Theoretical Account of the Afterlife (2022) Science, Vol. 1, pp. 55-58

[2] A. L. Snesenon - Applied Soul-Searching (2022) MIT press

[3] G. Brompton, S. Ekebo, W Brunner - A Parallel Universe for Quantum Souls (2022) Proceedings of the National Academy of the Sciences, Vol. 4, pp. 123-134

[4] E. Andropov, B. Green, M. L. Strauss - Metaverse Versus Parallel Universe: Logical Implications of Sub-Threshold Oscillations in the Snesenon Field (2023) Physica E, Vol. 20, pp. 567-588

[5] A. L. Snesenon - Canonical Faith Physics (2023) Oxford University Press

[6] Guess Who's Laughing Now? (2024) Vatican Press

[7] Potifex Maximus Pius Secundus - Exsuge Hic Richardus Dawkinsus (2025) Papal Encyclical

[8] H. Zeng, S. Kazaw-Fourthegg - Methodological Advances in Science 1: Prayer (2025) Cambridge University Press

[9] M. Nachtmann, S. Kazaw-Fourthegg - Methodological Advances in Science 2: Private Revelations (2025) Cambridge University Press

[10] B. R. Snuseg, B. Shud - Psychological Dogmas Versus Neuroscience Fatwas: A Modelling Study (2026) Psychological Review, Vol. 55, pp. 898-998

[11] S. Hawking - The False Induction Paradox (2026) Nature, Vol. 562, pp. 234-250

[12] S. B. P. Son - God's Quiver (2026) Advances in Faith Physics and Theology, Vol. 13, pp. 127-230

[13] A. H. Femo - Finally Something to Do. Or, Why God Delegates Supervision (2026) Advances in Faith Physics and Theology, Vol. 13, pp. 231-239

[14] M. S. Pidd - Divine Transmutation of Human Waste Gases (2027) Journal of Applied Theology, Vol. 43, pp. 677-699

[15] P. Samma - Do They Eat? - On the Nature of Soul Excrement (2028) Journal of Applied Theology, Vol. 43, pp. 700-720

[16] M. A. Jolean, P. H. Soja - Deriving an Upper Limit for the Number of Martyrs: on the Constant Replenishing of the 72 (2030) Proceedings of the ISS, Vol. 1, pp. 342-401

[17] R. Bennett, N. Brunel - On the Distribution of Representatives of Different Faiths in the Beyond Compared to Self-Reported Affiliation in Life - Three Case Studies of Sudden Death (2030) Journal of Statistical Faith Physics, Vol. 1, pp. 555-732

[18] C. Hitchens (departed) - Even if He Runs the Show, He Is Still Not Great (2031) Afterlife Press

[19] S. C. H'Nuki – On the "Mother-in-law syndrome" (2031) Faith Physics Review E, Vol. 4, pp. 55-73

[20] J. Hybsi, A. Norber - Matching 'the Voices in the Head' to Known Snesenon Signatures: Schizophrenia as a Gateway to the Afterlife (2031) Nature Snesenology, pp. 222-454

[21] Dalai Lama - Upper Bounds for the Time in the Beyond Before Reincarnation. (2031) Journal of Mathematical Snesenology, Vol. 99, pp. 646-678

[22] Dalai Lama - Reincarnation Provides the Best Fit to Snesenon Engine Data (2032) Feel Good Press

[23] D. O. Godore - Mathematical Constraints on Reincarnation During the Late Heavy Bombardment (2032) International Journal of Snesenology - Special Issue on Reincarnation. Pp. 789-799

[24] G. W. Leibniz - Novo methodus pro maximis et minimis, itemque tangentibus, quae nec fractas nec irrationales quantitates moratur, et singulare pro illis calculi genus (1684)

[25] I. Newton - Philosophiæ Naturalis Principia Mathematica (1687)

[26] G. W. Leibniz - Essais de Théodicée sur la bonté de Dieu, la liberté de l'homme et l'origine du mal (1720)

[27] L. Otobo, D. Ziem - Demon Theory (2033) Journal of a Morality, Vol. 44, pp. 90-99

[28] I. D. Toi, M. Noro - Advanced Free Will Theory of Evil (2033) Theologica F, Vol. 6, pp. 55-55

[29] S. Ham, A. A. Moth - A Combined Model WTF and DT (2033) Creation Press

[30] The Bible - Leviticus 14:4-7, King James Version

[31] A. Prunitos - Matching Sumerian Phonemes to Cuneiform Script (2034) Journal of Advanced Seal Science, Vol. 562, pp. 1-37

[32] P. Robertson, S. Ham - On the Misinterpretation of the Comedic Efforts of So-Called Creationists (2034) Darwin Press

[33] C. Springtime, R. M. F. Caust - The Common Sense Paradox (2034) Journal of Absolute Morality, Vol. 666, pp. 13-17

[34] Z. Zycra - An Alternative Derivation of the Snesenon Equations (2034) Journal of Theoretical Faith Physics, Vol. 78, pp. 234-245

[35] Z. Zycra, A. L. Snesenon - Extensions to Quantum Soul Physics: The Regress Field (2035) Science, Vol. 5, pp. 354-37

[36] Z. Zycra - Engineering the Snesenon effect Zero Point to Build a New Type of Snesenon Engine (2037) Journal of Applied Snesenology. Vol. 6, pp. 898-1005

[37] Z. Zycra - New Approaches to Quantum Soul Theory: Theory and Applications (2027) Doctoral Thesis - Central European University

[38] M. V. Laziale, C. Dalongelo - A Unifying Theory of the Afterlife (2037) arxiv.org

Afterword

In satire irony is militant, a critic once said. I did my best to obey this rule. My sole motivation for writing this short book was to give form to a crazy idea and to have fun in the process. In order not to offend the fictitious soul of Bertrand Russell, I stress that I do not claim originality concerning all of the arguments presented here. Many have been expressed before by various critics of religion. I also wish to acknowledge some sources of inspiration explicitly. First, the title of Chapter 18 (Summa Technologiæ) is (aside from the obvious play on Aquinas' Summa) an homage to the book with the same title by the great Stanislaw Lem. Second, the part of the same chapter which touches on one of Aquinas' proofs of God has been partially inspired by the corresponding chapter in Richard Dawkins' *God Delusion*. Third, the quote I attribute to Bertrand Russell 'I was wrong! God's plan does indeed involve Hitler, the holocaust, and the A-bomb!' is, of course, a deliberate inversion of his own words found in his book *Why I am not a Christian*.

Concerning the chapter on Plato and the Old Testament: I am aware that later Christianity is heavily influenced by Greek ideas and is often seen as the (unfortunate?) marriage of Middle-Eastern monotheism and Greek metaphysics. Nevertheless, the difference in outlook on the world between the Old Testament and the contemporary wider Greek world is startling, which is the main idea I wanted to express in that chapter.

Finally, I wish to thank friends and family who have patiently read the manuscript and given feedback. You all know who you are. Very special thanks go to two people. Maria Elena Fernandez for editing and typesetting this paperback version, and for inventing the crazy union's manifesto. Soren Bendt Pederson for his wonderful cover design and his enthusiasm. If you read this far, go check out his website of amazing concept art.

London, 04.10.2017
Andrej Bičanski

*****

About the Author

Andrej Bičanski is a physicist turned neuroscientist, working as a researcher in London, UK. As far as fiction is concerned the Faith Physics novella is his debut work. More is to come.

Made in the USA
Coppell, TX
08 December 2020

43842227R00095